THE RAYNE TOUR
BOOK #1

ALWAYS
WATCHING

Brandilyn Collins & Amberly Collins

ALWAYS WATCHING

BOOK ONE

the Rayne Tour

ZONDERVAN®

For the *real* Brittany

☙

ZONDERVAN

Always Watching
Copyright © 2009 by Brandilyn Collins

This title is also available as a Zondervan ebook.
Visit www.zondervan.com/ebooks.

Requests for information should be addressed to:
Zondervan, 3900 *Sparks Dr. SE, Grand Rapids, Michigan 49546*

This edition: ISBN-978-0-310-74918-9

Library of Congress Cataloging-in-Publication Data

Collins, Brandilyn.
        Always watching / by Brandilyn and Amberly Collins.
             p. cm. — (Rayne Tour series ; bk. 1)
        Summary: When a frightening murder occurs after one of her famous mother's
rock concerts, sixteen-year-old Shayley tries to help the police find the killer and to
determine whether her long-lost father has some connection to the crime.
        ISBN 978-0-310-71539-9 (softcover)
        [1. Murder—Fiction. 2. Single-parent families—Fiction. 3. Rock groups—Fiction.
4. Fame—Fiction. 5. Mystery and detective stories.] I. Collins, Amberly. II. Title.
PZ7.C692AI 2009
        [Fic]—dc22   2008039515

Published in association with the literary agency of Alive Communications, Inc., 7680 God-
dard Street, Suite 200, Colorado Springs, CO 80920. www.alivecommunications.com.

Interior design: Christine Orejuela-Winkelman

Printed in the United States of America

15 16 17 18 19 20 21 22 /DCI/ 20 19 18 17 16 15 14 13 12 11 10 9 8 7 6 5 4 3 2 1

Dear Reader,

When Zondervan asked if we'd like to collaborate as mother and daughter on a suspense series, we jumped at the chance. Before long our idea for the Rayne Tour Series was born. We both love music. And what better way to use our real-life experiences in attending concerts together than to write about a rock group?

We have pictures of us attending concerts going way back to when Amberly was in junior high. We always try to buy seats close to the front. We leap to our feet and scream and clap along with everyone else. We know what that crowd experience is like. The excitement, the energy. What would it be like, we wondered, to be backstage? To be a teenage girl with a rock star for a mom? All the money and fame and traveling. Is that kind of life pure fun and adventure — or does it bring challenges the rest of us never even think about?

And then — what if you threw a murder into the mix?

Our research for this first book in the series took us backstage at the HP Pavilion in San Jose, California. On that private tour we saw what the crowd doesn't see — the stage entrance, the dressing rooms, the special building exit for the performers. We heard stories about specific foods and furniture that musicians have requested in their contracts. We learned about security — something Shaley O'Connor is about to need more than ever …

As you read this story, we would love to hear from you. Please visit our shoutlife page at www.shoutlife.com/theraynetour.

~ Brandilyn and Amberly Collins

PART 1
Friday

PROLOGUE

It's not my fault I have to kill.

He'd been watching since the tour began. Eyes straight ahead, keeping cool, like he wasn't even paying attention. But he noticed everything. Even got a sense for what was happening behind his back. His past life had taught him how to do that — out of necessity. When it was something bad, he felt a vibration in the air, pulling up the hair on his arms. And he'd know. He'd just *know*.

Sometimes he acted behind the scenes. Nothing that would be noticed. Just ended up in a certain place at a certain time — a presence that kept the wrong thing from happening. Other times he'd say what needed to be heard. Real casual, not sounding like a threat at all. No, he was just talking, shooting the breeze about some previous experience. But beneath the words there'd be a point: *don't cross me or mine.*

Sometimes people were too dumb to get it. He'd give them every chance, trying to be the nice guy. Trying to do it the easy way. But no. Those kinds of people had stubborn minds and black hearts. Couldn't be trusted. They were headed for a fall and about to take some good people with them. *His* people.

That's what it had come to now.

"Hey, can I see you a sec before you go?" He motioned, and the one who must die came, humming.

Humming.

Like a lamb to slaughter.

1

The screams of twenty thousand people sizzled in my ears.

"Rayne, you reign! Rayne, you reign! Rayne, you reign!"

At the sold-out HP Pavilion in San Jose, California, the crowd chanted and clapped and stomped for my mom's group, Rayne—named after her—to do one more song before they left the stage. As usual I stood backstage with Tom Hutchens, my mom's twenty-five-year-old hairdresser and makeup artist and my closest friend on tour. Tom was short and slim, with thick black hair and an intense-looking face that didn't match his crazy personality at all.

Tom feigned the pucker of a hip-hop artist and splayed his fingers in front of his red T-shirt. "Yo, she reign, they go insane!" He had to shout at me, his Vans-clad feet dancing. Tom always wore these wild-looking sneakers with blue, white, and red checks and a red racing stripe on the sides. "Ain't nothin' plain about rockin' Rayne!"

I punched him in the arm, laughing. His silly rap rhymes were getting worse by the day.

With her blonde hair bouncing, Mom came flying down the steps on the way to her private dressing room for the two-minute break. Sweat shone on her forehead as she passed by. She flashed her red-lipped grin at me and raised a palm. We high-fived as she sped past.

"They love us, Shaley!"

"Course, Mom, they always do!"

The rest of the rock group — Kim, Morrey, Rich, and Stan — descended more slowly, their faces showing fatigue. None of them had the energy of my mother after a concert. Tom and I gave them a quick thumbs-up before scurrying after Mom.

As we hit the dressing room with Rayne O'Connor's name on the door, I checked my watch. 10:45. Yay! Almost time to head to the airport and pick up my best friend, Brittany. I hadn't seen her since Rayne started touring three months ago, and I couldn't *wait* to be with her again. This was Rayne's third tour, and I always found it hard to leave all my school friends behind.

Without Tom to keep me laughing, touring would be terribly lonely.

I walked in and closed the dressing room door, shutting out some of the noise.

"Whoo!" Mom crossed to the left side of the room and plopped into the makeup chair facing a long, brightly lit mirror. To her right sat a wooden armoire full of her clothing. She always changed outfits during intermission. Along the back wall were the blue sofa and matching armchairs specified by contract for her dressing area in every arena. Opposite the makeup counter was the table loaded with catered food, also specified by contract — bowls of fruit, sandwiches, pasta salad, cheese cubes, chips ... and M&M's for me.

Mom studied herself in the mirror with her large crystal blue eyes. "Okay, Tom, do your magic." She guzzled a drink from a water bottle on the counter.

Like she needed any magic. With her high cheekbones, oval face, and full lips, Mom was drop-dead gorgeous.

Tom winked at me as he snatched up a tissue. Sticking his scrawny neck out, he scrutinized Mom with animation — eyes narrowed and his mouth a rounded O. "Hm. Hmm."

He sighed, stood back, and spread his hands as if to say *nothing to be done here, you're perfect.*

Mom rolled her eyes at me. I shrugged. As if I could control Tom's antics.

"All right, lover boy." Mom took another swig of water. "Get to it! I've got one minute left."

"Yo, big Mama."

Mom swatted his hand. "Would you stop calling me that? I don't know why I put up with you." Her mouth curved.

Tom leaned in to blot her face with the tissue. "'Cause I make you look bodacious, that's why." Expertly, he retouched her blusher and lipstick and fluffed her hair.

Out in the arena, the crowd's yells and applause were growing louder. I smiled and squeezed Mom's shoulder. At every concert the fans went wild, but it never got old for me. Night after night their adoration made my chest swell with pride for my mom.

Five years ago when I was eleven and Mom was twenty-eight, Rayne was barely hanging on. Mom and the band played little concerts here and there, working night and day to get noticed. I remember how hard she tried back then. A great lyric writer with a distinct, throaty-edged voice, she deserved to make it big. Then the song "Far and Near" hit the radio, and after that—a rocket launch.

Tom stood back and surveyed Mom, his head cocked to one side. "Not bad. Not bad a-tall."

"Rayne, you reign! Rayne, you reign!" The crowd was going crazy out there.

Mom tossed her hair back and looked at herself from side to side. "Great." She sprang from the chair. "Gotta go." She hurried toward the door.

I moved out of her way. "Mom, don't forget, Tom and I are going to pick up Brittany in ten minutes. We're leaving a little early because Tom wants to stop by a drugstore."

"Oh, that's right." Mom pulled up short, one hand on the door knob. She looked to Tom. "Somebody else doing your cleanup?"

He glanced at me. "Got it taken care of."

Disappointment pulled at my mouth. Mom *knew* how I'd counted the days until Brittany's and my junior year of high school ended—just yesterday. My tutor had flown home this morning, and now Brittany was coming for two weeks. Mom was paying all her expenses — for that I was so grateful. But Mom could get so wrapped up in her work. Sometimes I just needed her to remember *me*.

Mom looked my way — and caught my expression. She smiled too wide, as if to make up for her distraction. "I'm so glad Brittany's coming, Shaley. We'll show her a great time."

I nodded.

"Mick's going with you, right?"

"Yeah."

Mick Rader had been my mom's main personal bodyguard for the past three years. The other two, Bruce Stolz and Wendell Bennington, would guard her on her way to the hotel tonight while Mick was with me.

"Okay, good. You'll be safe." Mom smiled as she opened the door. The crowd's screams rushed in. "See you at the hotel."

She blew me a kiss and disappeared.

The yelling suddenly frayed my nerves. I pushed the door shut and leaned against it.

Tom shot me his sad clown look, his lips turned down and eyebrows pulled into a V. He always read my mind so well.

I couldn't help but smile. "It's okay."

His expression whisked away. Tom struck his hip-hop pose. "Got a new one for ya."

"Oh, yeah?" I knew he'd come up with the lyrics as he went along, just to get me laughing again.

Tom's feet started their shuffle-dance. "Let's go for a ride down the avenue. Top down, windblown, my VW. The talk of the town in all we do. Shaley O'Connor puttin' on the view — "

He froze, mouth open, frowning hard. Then he jerked back into dancing. "Can't think of another line, can you?"

I giggled. "Great, Tom, as fabulous as all your others."

He bowed. "Thank ya, thank yaaa."

Pulling up straight, he glanced at the wall clock. "Yikes! I gotta take care of some things before the limo comes. Meet you at the back exit?"

"Okay."

As the door closed behind him, I crossed the room to check myself in the mirror. Excitement pulsed through my veins. Almost time to see Brittany! I chose a neutral lipstick and leaned toward the glass to apply it. Thanks to Tom, I'd learned a lot of makeup tricks, and my face needed little retouching. Finished with the lipstick, I ran a brush through my long brown hair. Tom had recently layered it and feathered the bangs. I liked the look.

Despite the difference in hair color, many people said I looked like my mother. I considered that a high compliment.

I stood back and turned side to side. Not bad. My new designer jeans fit well, and the blue top matched my eyes. Brittany would love the outfit. I grinned at myself, then glanced at the clock. Almost time for the limo to arrive.

In the arena, the crowd roared. Rayne was taking the stage. The first of two encore songs started — the band's new hit, "Do It Up Right."

For a few minutes I paced the room impatiently, munching M&M's. Rayne launched into their final song of the night.

Two hard knocks sounded on the door — Mick's signal. He stuck his square-shaped head inside. Mick is in his forties, ex-military. He has a thick neck and muscles out to *here*. Nobody messes with Mick. "Shaley, you ready?"

"Yes! Is the limo waiting?"

"Yeah." His deep-set brown eyes swept the room. "Where's Tom?"

"He said he had to take care of a few things. He'll meet us at the door." I crossed to the couch to pick up my purse.

"Okay. I'm going to stop in the bathroom, then I'll see you there." He gave me his squinty-eyed stare. "*Don't* step outside of the building without me."

I flicked a look at the ceiling. "Yeah, yeah." Mick was *so* protective. It's not like I'd be in any danger walking out that door.

As with all arenas where Rayne sang, the HP Pavilion had a special entrance for performers, guarded by the arena's own local security. And that whole section of the parking lot was roped off and guarded. No chance for any fans or paparazzi to sneak in.

Mick jabbed a finger at me for emphasis, then left.

Tingling with anticipation, I scurried out the door, intent on checking the other dressing rooms for Tom. *No time to wait, let's go, let's go!* Having been at the arena since four o'clock when sound checks began, I'd already learned the layout of the backstage area. There were eight dressing rooms — Mom's the biggest.

I hurried down the wide hall, mouthing "hi" to people I passed. The sound and light crews were still working, but the backline crew — the guys who maintain all the instruments and switch them out during performances — were done now. Set carpenters, managers, and all the people who tore down the stage milled around until the concert ended.

First I went to the back exit and peeked outside. Tom wasn't there.

I returned all the way up the hall, figuring I'd work my way back down.

For the first time, I noticed all the dressing room doors were closed. Strange. If Tom had gone into one to pack up something, he'd have left the door open as a courtesy. Those assigned rooms were personal space to members of the band and Rayne's production manager, Ross Blanke.

I peeked in the one next to Mom's.

Empty.

Shoving my purse handles higher up my shoulder, I went to the third.

Empty again.

The fourth.

No Tom.

This wasn't right. Tom was never late. Where was he?

Mick approached, signaling me with a roll of his finger — *let's get moving.*

I nodded. "Tom wasn't in the bathroom?"

Mick shook his head.

Together we walked to the fifth dressing room. Mick poked his head inside.

Empty.

I ran down to look in the sixth. No Tom.

I banged the door shut and looked around. What was going on? If he didn't show up soon, we wouldn't have time to go out of our way to a drugstore. The airport was minutes away from the arena. We didn't want Brittany waiting around by herself after dark.

"You take the next one." Mick strode past me. "I'll look in the one on the end."

The seventh dressing room had been allocated as Ross's office. At every venue, he needed a private area for calling people, dealing with last-minute problems, and basically seeing that everything in the contract was honored. I couldn't remember seeing Ross in the hall. He might be inside, and I didn't dare just barge in. The production manager's office was off-limits to everyone, unless invited.

I knocked and waited. Knocked harder.

No answer.

I opened the door.

Like Mom, Ross ordered the same room setup each time. For him that included an oversize desk with a black leather chair. On the desk he would stack his papers and folders, carefully position his laptop. A fax machine had to be on his left, a telephone with multiple lines on his right. Looking at Ross — a short, fat man with scraggly hair to his shoulders — you'd never guess what a neat freak he is.

And always on the wall — a large round clock.

As I stepped into the room, my eyes grazed that clock. 10:55. Brittany's plane would be landing soon.

On the floor beside the desk I glimpsed a splash of color.

Something twisted inside my stomach, almost as if my subconscious mind had already registered the sight. Time seemed to slow.

Clutching the door handle, I turned my head toward the color.

A foot. On the floor, sticking out from behind the desk. Wearing a Vans with blue, white, and red checks and a red racing strip. The foot lay on its side, toes pointed away from me, heel dug awkwardly into the carpet.

Deathly still.

2

I stared across the room at the foot. The back of my neck prickled. *Run*, my mind shouted. *Run and check on Tom!* But my feet rooted to the carpet, my fingers digging into the doorpost.

Onstage, the music stopped. Wild clapping and cheering rose from the arena.

The noise jerked me out of my zombie state. I lowered my purse from my shoulder and set it on the floor. Holding my breath, I crept forward.

As I edged around the side of the desk, Tom's jeaned leg came into view.

It wasn't moving.

My legs stopped.

"T-Tom?" My voice cracked into a whisper.

No answer.

So what? He couldn't have heard me above the crowd.

I took another step. Now I could see his second leg, drawn up and bent at the knee. Tom was lying on his side. I moved again and saw an arm flung out, fingers half curled toward the palm.

I leapt forward until his head came into sight. Tom's second arm lay crumpled against the carpet, his face partially turned into the short sleeve of his red T-shirt. His one visible eye was open, staring at the wall.

Air gushed out of my mouth. He was *tricking* me.

"You rotten thing!" I pushed at his leg with my toe. "How —"

No change. Just that wide-eyed stare.

All the relief that had spilled out of me reversed back down my throat. My windpipe closed until I could hardly breathe. I sank to my knees beside his chest.

"Tom?" I leaned down to look into both his eyes.

The other one was gone.

I mean *gone.* Just a black, bloody, gaping hole.

For the longest second of my life, all I could do was stare. It pulled at me, that hole. Like it wanted me to tumble inside it. A horror-film version of *Alice in Wonderland.*

Faintness gripped me. I swooned toward Tom's ravaged face, my nose almost touching where his eye used to be ...

At the last possible moment, my muscles jerked me back.

I shoved to my feet and screamed.

3

My shrieks bounced off the walls during the crowd's final shouts. In the next second all noise died away.

Silence rang in my ears.

I turned and ran.

Mick materialized in the doorway as I hurtled through it. I rammed into his rock-solid chest. With another scream I bounced off and collapsed on the carpet.

"What—?" Mick bent over me. I looked up, mouth flopping open. No sound came. I pointed a shaking finger toward Tom. Mick's head jerked up.

Horror crossed his face.

He jumped over me and ran to Tom, his hand reaching for the gun clipped to his belt.

Mick bent down and disappeared behind the desk. I couldn't get up. I couldn't do *anything*.

Voices of band members mingled in the hall, commenting on the performance. How strange the words sounded. So naïve. So *unknowing*.

Heavy footsteps approached. Ross rounded the corner and almost stepped on me.

"Ahhh!" I rolled away from him.

Mick rose up from behind the desk. Ross froze at the look on his face. "What's going on?"

"Tom's dead." Mick's voice was tight.

"*What?*"

"Somebody shot him."

Ross blinked rapidly, then leaped around me to see for himself.

Mick reached for the phone on the desk. "I'm calling 9 – 1 – 1."

I stared at the ceiling, my mind going numb. My limbs felt like water. Tom was dead. *Dead.* My heart couldn't grasp it. I'd just been with him. How could he be *gone*?

"Oh." The word choked from Ross's throat. He backed away from Tom.

"Yes," Mick said into the phone. "I need to report a homicide. Hang on a minute." He shoved the phone into Ross's hand. "You talk to them. I need to get Bruce and Wendell. We'll round up the band members, make sure they're safe."

Mom. Could whoever did this to Tom want to hurt *her*?

Mick ran past me, gun in hand. "Shaley, stay here."

I barely heard him. Panic pushed me onto weak knees. I had to find my *mother!*

Somehow I crawled out the door. "*Mom. Mommmm!*"

Every person in the hallway jerked around.

Mick spun back to me. "Shaley, stay *there!*" He swung toward the others. "Everyone, against the wall and *don't move*! Wendell, Bruce, where are you?"

People melted back, calling questions, their voices buzzing like a thousand bees in my head.

"Where's my mom?"

Bruce ran out of the men's bathroom, hand automatically going for his weapon. "*What?*" At six foot six, he has powerful, long legs and arms. I could see his head above everyone else's.

Wendell burst from the stage area. "Here!"

"Shaley?" Mom's sharpened voice filtered from up the hallway. "What's happening?" She came toward me, eyes wide.

"Rayne, stay where you are!" Mick shouted.

Mom picked up speed. Her head whipped back and forth, gawking at everyone pressed against the walls. She started to run. "Shaley, are you all right?

I teetered to my feet. "Tom's dead, Mom. He's *dead!*"

Gasps rose from dozens of throats. Mom didn't even slow. Mick grabbed her arm, but she yanked away. As if in a dream — a nightmare — I watched her tear-blurred form hurtle toward me. Mick, Bruce, and Wendell spread their feet, guns raised, eyes darting back and forth, searching the hall for danger.

I flung myself forward, sobbing.

After an eternity, Mom reached me. I collapsed into her arms, screaming Tom's name.

4

Time blurred into commotion and people and noise.

As the news spread, the arena's own security guards rushed backstage. Ross shoved my purse into my hands, and Mick herded me and Mom through chaos up the hallway and into her dressing room. Inside we sagged against the wall, my Mom white-faced and clinging to me as I cried. In minutes, uniformed San Jose police officers swarmed down on us, checking everyone's identities, clearing the hall, and securing the whole backstage area with yellow crime-scene tape. Plainclothes detectives arrived. The HP Pavilion's security force manned the doors and our private area of the parking lot.

All of us Rayne tour members were herded up to the Pavilion's concourse level, where suite after private suite opened up off the curving hallway. The band members and I huddled in one of those rooms. Policemen stood guard in the hall, spaced about two suites apart, talking now and then into the radios fastened to their uniforms.

Looking down over the arena, I could see the front rows of chairs already broken down and the wild scatter of containers for the instruments, lights, and sound equipment. Usually roadies would be hard at work, packing everything up. Local workers would be taking down the chairs. Now everything had just — stopped.

The band members tried to console me even in their own shock. Kim, Rayne's keyboard player and alto singer, could barely speak. Tom had been like a son to her. She hugged me hard, then stood back, long fingers sinking into her tanned forearms. Her heart-shaped face looked drawn, her heavy eye makeup smeared. "I'm so s-sorry you ... had to find him."

I could only nod.

Morrey, Rayne's drummer and Kim's boyfriend, slipped a tattoo-covered arm around her. He shook his head, full lips working but no sound coming out. He merely reached out a hand and laid it on my shoulder for a moment, his gold earring flashing in the overhead light. Towering over Kim, he bent his head down to hers, his shoulder-length black hair stark against her white-blonde.

Rich, the bass player, and Stan, lead guitarist, hugged Mom and me both. With his shaved head, square jaw, and piercing gray eyes, Rich had played small bad-boy parts in various movies. But I knew his heart.

"Sorry, Kitten," he whispered, his muscular arms around me. "I'm just so sorry."

I couldn't speak.

He pulled back, a strand of my hair catching on one of his huge diamond earrings. With a humorless smile, he untangled it.

Stan, born in America of African parents, gripped my shoulders and studied me with his coal-dark eyes. "We'll all be here for you, you know that."

My throat tightened. "Thanks."

Ross and two uniformed policemen came to our suite to talk to the band. Mom looked at me, one hand pressed against her cheek. "Let's go into one of the other rooms." She laid a hand on my head. "Shaley, stay here, okay? I'll be back soon."

I nodded.

After they all filed out, wooden and grim-faced, I closed the door. Like a lost child, I wandered a few steps toward the center of the room, then just stood there, hugging myself. Shivering.

My tears wouldn't stop.

Tom. On the carpet. His eye ... gone.

I couldn't grasp it. Couldn't believe it. My body was here, but my mind hovered, seeking a safe place to land. Just minutes before,

Tom had been singing one of his crazy rap songs. I was talking to him, laughing with him. How could someone *die* — just like that?

Who would do this? *Why?* Everybody loved Tom.

In my confused brain, Brittany's name suddenly surfaced. Oh, no! Somebody needed to go in the limo to pick her up at the airport. The police didn't want me to leave since I had found Tom. One of them would soon come to question me.

What happened to the limo, anyway?

I blinked at my watch. After eleven. Brittany's plane should have landed. Why hadn't she called?

Choking back my tears, I pulled my cell from my pocket and punched in her number.

Her voice mail immediately answered. Her phone was off.

Fresh panic gripped me. Had something happened to *her* too?

Maybe her plane was late.

With shaking fingers I pressed in her number again, praying she would answer. Telling myself this was stupid; planes were never on time these days.

The phone started to ring. I hunched over, smashing the phone against my ear. "Come on, Brittany, come on."

"Hey, you've reached Brittany. Call me ba — "

I choked out a sob. Snapped the phone shut.

My knees weakened. I stumbled over to a chair and fell into it.

A new kind of grief surged through me. I bent my head, shoulders shaking as I cried. Brittany *had* to be okay. I *needed* her now — so much. She'd been my best friend since second grade. Way before my mom and the band ever became famous. Way before *I* hit celebrity status as Mom's daughter. Now Brittany was the only friend I could talk to about certain things — like my deep yearning to know about my father and my resentment that Mom would never speak of him. Fame carried a heavy price. Now if I spoke of my unknown father with some other "friend," my intimate feelings just might end up on the cover of some national tabloid.

My nose started to clog, and my head ached. I tipped my chin up, brushing away tears, swiping hair from my face. I flipped my cell open, dialed 4 – 1 – 1 for the number to Southwest Airlines. Impatiently I listened to the company's automated answering system. I pushed the button to check arrival times.

What was her flight number?

I dug in my purse for the piece of paper with her flight and scheduled arrival, then pressed in the numbers, following the automated voice's instructions. Stupid thing. Why couldn't you talk to a real person?

Finally I heard my answer. Her plane was just landing.

Relief flowed through my veins, cold and biting. And right behind it — more pain over Tom.

I pushed off the couch. I had to find someone to ride in the limo and pick up Brittany. I didn't want some unknown driver doing it. Brittany would be upset enough when she heard what happened. She'd need someone to talk to —

A knock sounded on the door. I hurried toward it. "Yeah?"

Carly Sanders, my favorite of Rayne's three backup singers, opened the door before I could reach it. "Hey there, Shaley." Tears had tracked through the blusher on her black face.

"Hi." My chest constricted at the sight of her large, kind eyes. Carly had a way of looking not at me, but *through* me, as if she could read my soul.

She hugged me briefly but hard. "I came to tell you I'm going to pick up your friend at the airport."

"Oh, thanks. I was just going to find someone. Is the limo still here?"

"Yes. Mick took care of it."

Funny how unsettled that made me feel. People were always "taking care" of details for Mom and me. Suddenly, I didn't want that anymore. I wanted to take care of my own friend.

I wanted to find out who did this to Tom.

Carly put a hand underneath my chin. "I'm so sorry, Shaley. How *awful* for you. I know what a friend Tom was to you."

Was.

My face crumbled.

Carly pulled me close again and patted my back, crooning like a mother to her baby. "Poor child. Jesus, help her. Only your power and strength can help Shaley get through this."

Carly talks as openly about God as Mom talks about publicity, but I'd never heard her pray for me before. It felt strange but good.

I pulled back, wiping at the tears. "You'd better leave."

"Yeah."

I stepped into the doorway to watch her go. To the left of the threshold stood the ever-brooding Bruce, feet apart and arms folded. Solid as a mountain.

"Hi." I sniffed. "Didn't know you were here."

Like Mick, Bruce had served in the Marines. His hands and feet are huge, his face all stark angles with deep-set brown eyes. With his blond hair in a ponytail and a trimmed goatee, he looks like a hairy version of Lurch from the old *Addams Family* reruns. Like Lurch, he rarely smiles.

"I'm always here for you, Shaley."

"Yeah, I know."

That new resentment stirred within me once more — irrational, but there it was. Mom and I, as well as the rest of the band, *needed* to be guarded. Especially now. But I didn't want to be cut off from the world. I wanted to *do* something. I wanted to fight back against the evil that had happened to us.

"You okay?" Bruce asked.

I looked at the floor. "No."

He nodded. "I'm sorry. It's a shock. Wish I'd found him instead of you."

Me too.

I turned to look down the wide curving hallway. Carly was about to round the corner out of sight. From the other direction came Jerry Brand, one of our bus drivers. He nodded kindly to Carly as she passed.

Stage manager Pete Strickland, in charge of all logistics — traveling to a new venue, setting up, loading out — appeared farther down the hall and spoke to an officer. Pete's thin lips and hooked nose had earned him the nickname *Hawk*. He was like a hawk too, always keeping an eye on everything that happened. Most likely he was now questioning when we could leave. He and the officer spoke for a moment before Pete turned to talk to Jerry.

Memories of the yellow crime-scene tape tugged at me. On TV it seemed so benign. In real life it looked brutal.

What was happening backstage?

Was Tom still in Ross's office, lying on the floor? I thought of all the crime shows I'd seen, people plucking stray hairs and pieces of lint from the body. Taking pictures, discussing the corpse's temperature and position, theorizing how and when the murder had occurred.

How cold and inhuman. He wasn't Tom anymore; he was just a mound of evidence waiting to be hauled to the morgue.

My stomach flip-flopped.

Who had done this to him? *Why?*

I leaned against the doorjamb, gazing at nothing, mounting anger mixing with my pain. Somebody had killed Tom. That person needed to *pay*.

And I was going to do everything I could — and more — to make sure that happened.

Lifting my chin, I stepped into the hallway, set on asking the nearest policeman to radio someone backstage. I wanted to know what they were doing down there.

5

S haley, where you going?" Bruce demanded.
I didn't look back. "To talk to that policeman."
"You're supposed to stay here."
"I don't care."
A deep sigh seeped from his throat. I heard his heavy footsteps following.
Down the hall, Jerry Brand saw me coming and cut off his conversation with Pete. Jerry started toward me, glancing at the officer as he passed. He met me halfway, planting his short, stocky body in my path. I halted. Behind me, Bruce's footsteps stopped.
"Hey, Shaley." Jerry's voice was gentle. "I was just about to come see how you're doing."
Despite his obvious goal to stop me, the genuine concern in his voice squeezed my heart. His green eyes studied me, his forehead wrinkled. In his fifties, Jerry wore a black Rayne T-shirt, his belly hanging over the waist of his loose-cut jeans. He gave me his trademark crooked smile, although this one was sad. "You look like you've been through a lot."
I nodded.
Under the lights, Jerry's bald crown looked sallow. He latched his hands behind his back, put his weight on one leg, and thrust the other one forward. His eyes rose briefly over my shoulder to Bruce. "I know you got a lot of help here, but I just ... wondered if there's anything I can do."
The word *no* formed on my tongue, then dissolved. As awkward

as he appeared in asking, Jerry clearly wanted to help. I forced a tiny smile of my own. "In the next few days I just might need another one of your wild hunting stories."

His round face brightened. "Oh yeah? The fish so big it pulled me outta the boat?"

"You know I've heard that a dozen times."

"The bear that chased me through the woods when I was stalking a deer?"

In spite of myself, my smile widened. "I like that one. Brittany's coming tonight, you know. She'll love to hear it."

Three men in the HP Pavilion's security-guard uniform appeared and spoke with the policeman. They spotted me and turned their backs, talking in low tones.

Jerry glanced around at them, then nodded at me, satisfied. "Okay. You got it. Maybe in Denver. We're pulling out at six a.m."

We meant the tech bus and the huge trucks that carried all the equipment. "Wow, that will be hard. You'll be tired." Normally he and Vance, the driver he switched off with, would be sleeping now. While on the road, the driver's job was the hardest. At least the technicians on the bus could sleep in their beds all day if they wanted. Jerry only got to rest on his bunk when Vance drove.

Jerry shrugged. "It's what I was hired for."

"How long's the drive?"

"About twenty hours. That's without stops to eat. So probably more like twenty-three. We'll get there about six o'clock Sunday morning. Denver time."

What a life. I was glad I got to stay in hotels and fly everywhere. All day tomorrow, while the buses and trucks were driving, the band had a free day at the hotel.

"Okay, Jerry. See you there. And thanks for coming to check on me."

"No problem."

I made a move to pass him.

"Shaley." Bruce's low voice sounded behind me. "Don't."

Jerry held his hands up, palms out. "I don't think you want to be going anywhere, Shaley. That suite's for your own protection."

Irritation wriggled in my gut. "I just want to talk to the policeman. Hear what they're doing downstairs."

"They're doing their job. Collecting evidence."

"But maybe they'll miss something. I need to make sure."

"Listen." Jerry laid a hand on my shoulder. "You want to help? This isn't the way. The best thing you can do is remember every detail when the police interview you. They'll be counting on you for that."

Jerry's gaze lifted above my head. I could imagine Bruce nodding to him in agreement.

Before I could reply, the door to the suite nearest the officer and security guards opened. Mom appeared, Mick alongside. She caught my eye and began walking toward me with purpose. In her concert clothes — the straight-legged jeans and red high heels, an Ella Moss top — she looked every bit the star, even though her face was grim, her usually lithe movements tense. The policeman ogled her as she passed. Mick gave him a hard look.

Jerry glanced around and saw her coming. He stepped out of her way.

Mom drew up, her expression pinched.

"Shaley, let's go in there." She pointed to the suite where I'd been. "We need to talk."

6

All around the arena, red lights ripped the night, slashing across the countless police officers scurrying here and there with such self-importance. He leaned against the glass, looking down on all the activity. From here in the soundproof building he could hear nothing. But he imagined the shouts and police radios and car doors slamming.

All this chaos — thanks to *him*.

He smiled.

A policeman strode by, talking into the radio attached to his shoulder.

He stifled a laugh. All these uniforms hustling around looking for a killer — and there he stood. Right in front of their faces.

He'd already given his statement to one police officer. He'd seen nothing, knew nothing.

Cops were morons. Not to mention unjust. In his previous existence, they'd liked nothing better than putting him behind bars. First time at age sixteen. He hadn't deserved that.

Last time he got out, he'd vowed it — no more jail. Never again. For by then he had a new mission in life. He'd been sent to watch the Special One.

He slipped parole and secured a new identity. Now his past was wiped clean.

"Hey." One of his fellow workers appeared beside him, arms folded and pulled tightly to his chest. Guy looked nervous. "This is insane, isn't it?"

"Totally."

"I can't believe this happened."

"Me either."

Down below, a new police car carved to a stop outside the building. The driver's door opened, and a cop hurried out.

"It's so terrible." The man next to him sighed. "Poor Tom."

"Yeah. Poor Tom."

He ran a hand over his mouth, hiding his smile.

7

Nerves prickling, I followed Mom into the suite. She sat down on the couch, patted the cushion beside her. I sank into it.

Mick took up residence just outside the door. Opposite him I could see Bruce's trouser leg and one huge dangling hand. Doubly guarded.

Without a word, Mom hugged me. I leaned against her, soaking in her comfort.

She let me go too soon.

I clutched my hands. "What are they doing down there? It's taking forever."

"They're gathering evidence. That's all I know."

"Why aren't they talking to *me*? I'm the one who found him. I'm the one who saw him last."

"They're about to. A detective's coming up here in a minute. He'll want to hear everything."

I firmed my mouth. "It's about time."

Mom thrust her long red fingernails into her hair. "Look, I know this is a terrible time to talk about this, but a lot is happening at once. You need to know we may have to stop the tour."

I blinked. The tour had been the last thing on my mind. "Why?"

She lifted a hand. "It's in every contract that we can cancel venues if some disaster happens. And this certainly qualifies."

"You mean we might just stop everything and go home?"

"I don't know. Ross has to figure it out."

I stared at her. "That's what you all were talking about in there? The *tour*?"

"Like I said, it's a bad time." She rubbed her temple. "But it's reality."

"Maybe it is reality, but—*already*? I thought you all were in there talking about Tom. Who might have killed him—"

"We *were*, Shaley."

"Obviously not for very long."

"Why are you snapping at me?" Her voice sharpened.

Tears bit my eyes. "Because it sounds like you don't even care."

"Of *course* I care."

"About what? Tom or the tour?"

Mom looked away from me, mouth tightening. I folded my arms and glared at her.

"Look," she said after a minute. "I know you're upset. You've had a terrible shock. Please don't take that out on me. We need to stick together here."

I focused on my lap. A tear dropped down, wetting a circle on my jeans. "I'm sorry. I just ..."

She sighed. "I know."

I rubbed a thumb against the damp spot.

Mom's voice edged. "Listen, Shaley, if there's anything I'm worried about most, it's you. Danger came far too close to you tonight. When I think that you might have been with Tom when he walked into that office—" Her words cut off. Mom's jaw squared, and she blinked hard a few times. "So here's the deal. You're not going *anywhere* without a bodyguard. I mean *nowhere*. Not one step out of your hotel room, understand? Not *one step* into the parking lot."

I nodded.

Mom took a deep breath and ran a hand over her face. "Have you heard from Brittany?"

"She should be calling any minute."

We'd planned to have so much fun. Now what a nightmare she was walking into.

I drew in my shoulders. "Who do you think did this?"

Mom shook her head. "It has to be a local stagehand. I just can't believe it could be one of our own people. Arena security knows every person they let in that back door. They'll find him, Shaley. Whoever it is, they'll catch him."

"But why would someone who didn't even know Tom come in and kill him?"

"I don't know. That's what I keep asking myself. Ross couldn't see that anything had been taken from his office."

A huge man with short-cropped dark hair materialized in the doorway. My breath hitched.

Mom patted my leg. "It's the detective." She started to rise. "Come in."

I gawked at him. He looked like an ex-linebacker after a fifty-pound weight gain.

The man held up a hand. In his other one he carried a notebook. "That's okay, don't get up." He lumbered over to a chair against the wall and picked it up like a matchstick. Brought it over to set in front of us. When he sat down, it squeaked beneath his weight.

He gave me a little smile. His face was square and rugged with a flat nose.

"Shaley, I'm Detective Furlow with the San Jose Police Department." He raised thick eyebrows, and his forehead wrinkled. "I've gotten all the immediate information I can from Mick, but now I need to talk to you. Since you saw Tom first, you're an important witness."

Finally — something I could *do*. "I know. I'm ready."

He tapped his shirt pocket. "I have a little tape recorder that I'm going to turn on before we start. Okay? It'll pick up your voice from here. " He pushed a button on the recorder, then stated his name, our names, and the time — 11:45.

Had it only been an hour since I counted the minutes to get Brittany? It seemed a *lifetime* ago. Everything was planned then. Everything was *safe*.

"Shaley, when did you last see Tom?"

"He was in Mom's dressing room. We were getting ready to go to the limo and pick up my friend at the airport. He said he had a few things to do and that he'd meet me at the exit."

"Know what time that was?"

"Around ten forty-five."

"Do you have any idea what he was going to do when he left that room?"

I raised a shoulder. "Not really. I just figured he was packing stuff up."

The detective jotted a note. "Have any idea why he went into the production manager's office? I hear it's not typical for anyone other than Ross Blanke to be in there."

"I have no idea. I wondered the same thing."

"Did you trust Tom, Shaley?" Detective Furlow's voice was gentle.

I nodded, fresh tears pooling in my eyes. Mom put her hand on my knee.

"Were you friends?"

"Yes." I hated that word — *were*. "We teased around all the time. He was with me and Mom a lot, doing our hair and makeup. He was just ... really fun to be with." My words trailed away.

My brain conjured up the picture of Tom on the floor. His fingers curled toward his hand. The black hole for an eye. I shuddered a breath. "Mom says one of the local stagehands must have done it."

"Maybe. Don't know yet."

"You can know *that*. *Nobody* on our tour would want to hurt Tom. Everybody loved him."

"Okay."

"Besides, there are certain people you can *know* didn't do it. Like the band. They were all onstage."

Even before the last word left my mouth, I realized that wasn't true. Tom had left the dressing room before I heard the first of Rayne's two encores start up.

Well, that didn't matter. No one in the band would have done this.

The detective watched me as if reading my thoughts.

"It's *true*." My voice rose. "Nobody I know would have wanted to hurt Tom."

Detective Furlow's eyes moved to Mom's face, then back to mine.

I straightened. "What *do* you know? Did you find the gun?"

He surveyed me, as if deciding how much to say. "I have a daughter your age. I can't imagine what this would be like for her."

I leaned forward, seizing my chance. "I'll tell you what it would be like. She'd want to know everything she could, because she'd want the person who did this to her friend found and sent to jail. So — *did* you find the gun?"

He dipped his chin. "Yes. In the top drawer of the desk."

My eyes widened. I hadn't really expected him to say yes. "Why there? It can't be Ross's."

"Quickest way to get rid of it, I suppose."

I pulled my top lip between my teeth, trying to picture someone shooting Tom, stashing the gun in the desk, and slipping from the room. With *so many* people around. Whoever did it had nerves of steel.

"But why didn't we hear the shot?"

The detective cleared his throat. "The gun had a silencer."

A silencer. Like someone had *planned* this.

"Well, if you have the gun, *and* a silencer, can't you find out whose it is then?"

Detective Furlow gave me a wan smile as if to say, *you watch too much TV.* "We've bagged the weapon. Unfortunately, the identifying numbers on the gun have been filed down. Maybe we can make out a few of them in the lab. But it's not likely a legally owned weapon anyway."

Frustration bounced around in my chest. "So that won't help you find the guy?"

"Maybe, if we can identify it enough to track down where it came from. But it'll take time."

"We don't *have* time. We need to find the answers *now!*"

My cell phone went off — Brittany's ring tone. Distractedly, I flipped open the phone. "Hi."

"Shaley, why didn't *you* come? What's going *on?*"

My eyes flicked to the detective, then Mom. "I can't talk now. Just get here. I'll tell you everything."

"This is scaring me. *You're* scaring me. Are you okay?"

"Yes. No. I don't know."

"What kind of answer is that?"

"Is Carly there?"

"Yes. The driver's loading my bag in the limo."

"She'll tell you what happened. And you'll be here soon. It's not far."

"Shaley, what — "

"Brittany, I have to go. See you soon."

I snapped the phone closed. "Sorry."

"No problem."

The detective continued asking me questions. I related what I was doing before I found Tom. What rooms I looked into first. Where Mick searched. Then I had to describe what I saw. Did I move Tom in any way? Touch him?

The question sent a shudder up my spine. "For a minute I thought he was teasing me." *If only.* "I pushed him with my foot. But that didn't ... move him."

The detective asked me what I knew about Tom's friends. Who was he close to on the tour? Did he have any enemies? Had he gotten into any fights with anybody recently?

"No." I hugged myself. "Like I said, everyone loves him." I winced. *Loved him.*

Out in the hall, I heard a familiar voice. Brittany had arrived. I sprang to my feet, but felt pulled in two directions.

"My friend is here. Can I see her just a minute?"

Detective Furlow closed his notebook. "Go ahead, we're done for now, Shaley."

"You sure?" I glanced out the door. "I want to help all I can."

Mom stood up. The detective did the same. He towered above me. "Don't worry, I'll be around. I'm going to be right here for a while, talking to your Mom."

"Okay." With a quick look at Mom, I scurried across the room and into the hallway. Brittany stood close to the door, whispering with Mick. She'd hung around with me enough back home to know our bodyguards.

"Brittany!"

She rushed at me. We hugged each other hard.

I pulled back and looked at her, starting to shake. The mere sight of her brought tears to my eyes. "You look *great*." She'd cut new layers in her long blonde hair, and the makeup on her hazel eyes was perfect.

She scrutinized me through her thick, long lashes. "Are you *okay*? Carly told me what happened. I just can't believe it."

"I'm ... yeah." Words tangled in my head. So much to tell her. I didn't know where to begin.

Pete Strickland reappeared up the hall, followed by Ed Husker,

Rayne's sound tech. They headed our direction. *Great. More people.* "Come on, Brittany." I took her arm. "Let's go somewhere to talk."

I hauled her two suites down, Bruce heavy on our heels. We passed Wendell, standing guard at the suite next door, where the other band members and Ross had gathered. Wendell's arms were folded, a tight T-shirt showing off his rocklike muscles. At five eleven, he's the shortest of our bodyguards but intimidates me the most. His black hair, two inches long and gelled, stands straight up. His eyes are deep-set and hard. A long shiny scar runs the length of his chin.

Briefly, he nodded to me. I nodded back.

In the third suite, the atmosphere hung heavy and dark. Carly sat on a couch along with the two other backup singers.

I stopped just inside the door. "Is it okay if we just sit over there and talk?" I pointed to the front corner of the room.

"Sure," Carly said. "Brittany, you remember Lois and Melissa?"

Lois is tall and skinny with short brown hair. Melissa is a large African American who sings like an angel but hardly says a word. Brittany had met them and all the other band members before at our house, but it had been a while since they'd seen each other.

"Yeah." Brittany managed a smile. "Hi."

"Hi," Lois said. Melissa nodded.

Brittany and I sank onto the carpeted floor. Quickly I told her the details. Her eyes filled with tears. She took my hands in hers. "Shaley —"

Ross poked his head in the suite. His pudgy face was flushed. The large diamond ring on his right hand glittered in the overhead light as he gripped the doorpost. "Lois, Melissa, Carly, come on next door. We need to talk about the tour." He flicked a look at Brittany and me, then disappeared. Carly gave us a tight smile as she and the other two women filed from the room.

Brittany bit her lip. "You think he's going to stop the tour?"

Canceling would make Tom's death doubly hard. Local promoters would have to be reimbursed their advance fees. Ticket sales would be paid back. Ross, Mom, the whole band, the technicians and roadies, *everybody* would be out a lot of money.

"I don't think so." My voice was tight. "I know Ross. He'll be thinking about the bottom line. He'll say we still have Marshall to do Mom's hair and makeup. I don't mean to say Ross is cold, but the fact is — it's not like one of the band members is dead."

Pain stabbed through me. The tour might physically be able to continue, but how could I manage the rest of it without Tom? Especially after Brittany left.

Brittany picked at the carpet. "It'll be over for *me* for sure. When Mom hears this, she'll want me on the next plane home. Count on it — I'll be leaving tomorrow."

My eyes widened. "Brittany, no! I *need* you here!" I hadn't had time to think about it, but she was so right. Brittany's mom was very strict. We'd had to beg her to let Brittany come in the first place.

"I know." Brittany's focus drifted over my shoulder, as if she saw something in the distance. Fear flicked across her face. Her mouth opened, then closed. She pressed her lips in the expression I knew all too well.

I leaned forward. "What is it?"

For as long as I'd known Brittany she'd had an uncanny ability to sense things. Not often, nor predictably. But when the sensing came, she always turned out to be right.

She shook her head.

"Come on, *what*?"

Brittany turned troubled eyes on mine. "I feel something."

Her fear curled up in my stomach. "I know. Tell me what it is."

She bit her lip, studying me. "I'll just say this: we *have* to persuade Mom to let me stay."

9

This is not right.

Anger had started to bubble inside him, acid eating at his insides. All these cops. All the chaos and worry and tears. As if Tom's life had been worth something.

He had to hide it, this anger of his. He had responsibilities. People to talk to, decisions to make. Not to mention the monster man detective — Furlow — was about to question him.

This would not be a problem. No detective was going to trip him up.

He watched two cops conferring, his mind spinning back to the day he got out of prison. "Good luck," a guard had told him as he walked out to freedom. He'd just smiled. Luck? He didn't need it. He had his superior intelligence — and a purpose. A service to perform.

For the right amount of money, of course.

"Hey!" An officer swaggered over. They all swaggered. Thought they were so powerful. "Detective Furlow wants to see you now."

"Sure."

He turned and walked confidently toward his second session with the cops.

Over and over I asked Brittany what she'd sensed. But she refused to tell me. That ticked me off, and I told her so. As if I didn't have enough on my mind already. As if I wanted to fight with my best friend.

"Shaley," she finally huffed. "I don't *know* exactly what's going to happen, okay? Only that you need me with you this week. Because the tour's going to continue, and without me ... there's danger."

"There was danger before you got here. Obviously."

"I mean danger for you. Personally."

"We have three bodyguards; what are *you* gonna do?"

"I don't *know*! But you kept bugging me so I told you what I felt. Stop taking it out on me."

A huge sigh deflated my chest. I slumped over and stared at the carpet. "Sorry. I'm just ... This is all so ..."

"I know."

Shortly before one o'clock, Mom came into the room, looking haggard. "Girls, we've been released to go to our hotel. The limos are waiting at a side door, and our suitcases have been loaded. Come on."

I pushed to my feet, muscles prickly from sitting cross-legged too long. "What about the tour?"

"We're going on with it," she said tersely.

I exchanged a grim look with Brittany.

As we slid into our limo, guarded all around by policemen, her words trailed through my mind. *Danger for you ...*

Kim, Morrey, and Carly got into the stretch limo with me, Mom, and Brittany. Bruce and Wendell climbed in last. The rest of the band went into a second car. As usual, Ross had gone ahead to check everyone into the hotel. Some of the personal attendants and others who traveled with the band drove with him. The driver shut the door behind us, and seconds later we began to roll out of the parking lot.

I pushed Brittany's warning out of my head. It was only a threat if she didn't stay. But she would — we'd make sure of that. Brittany couldn't literally protect me. But we had plans while she was here. Maybe what she'd sensed would only happen if we couldn't follow through with those plans.

"Oh, great." Mom peered forward through the windshield. "*Look* at the crowd."

Outside the protected area of the HP Pavilion parking lot reporters swarmed. As our limo crept forward, they descended upon us like wasps. Policemen fought them back with little success. Camera flashes split the night. Voices yelled my name.

Me? I turned wide eyes to Mom.

She put an arm around me, whispering, "They've heard you found him."

I leaned into her. I hated these types of crowds. Even when separated from me by a car, the crush of people snatched air from my lungs.

Brittany cringed on my left, hands shoved between her knees. "Where did they all come from?"

Morrey made a sound in his throat. "They never sleep."

Television camera lights surged on, spilling over shouting mouths and microphones, a man being shoved back by police, a disembodied hand holding a still camera high. Beyond the lights, dark shadows played over faces and shoving bodies, turning them grotesque and malformed.

Something pummeled the window. I screamed. Brittany sank her fingernails into my arm.

"It's okay, girls." Mom's voice sounded tight. "They can't get in. We'll be through this in a minute."

"It'll be all over the news tomorrow." Kim sat straight, unaffected. She was fearless in crowds. "You wait. I'm talking *every channel. All day.*"

We pulled away from the crowd onto the street. Our limo picked up speed.

"My mom will hear." Brittany's breath hitched. "She'll make me go home."

"Mom, *do* something," I begged. "Brittany *can't* leave."

Onstage, Rayne O'Connor always looked confident and beautiful. A bundle of dancing, singing energy, feeding off the crowds. Now the corners of her mouth drew down, and her eyes were bloodshot.

She patted my leg. "I'll call Linda tonight, even though it's late." Mom leaned forward to look at Brittany. "I promise — I'll get her to let you stay."

Brittany let out a hopeful sigh. If anyone could accomplish that, it was my mom. Hard to say no to Rayne O'Connor.

At the hotel, Wendell, Bruce, and Mick hustled us in a side door and up to our rooms. We met Ross on our private floor for our room keys and the night's "code" — a list of names and room numbers, plus the password. For protection and privacy, only those in our party and a few key people on the buses had the code. Anyone else calling the hotel and asking to be put through to one of our rooms would be denied.

"You're not leaving your room tomorrow, understand?" Mom said as a bellman opened her door for her and lugged in suitcases.

For weeks, Brittany and I had planned to go shopping on Saturday. I thought again of Brittany's warning to me — the plans we should keep. At least that's the way I interpreted it. Tomorrow would be plenty soon enough to argue with Mom about shopping. I could wear a disguise, and we'd have a bodyguard with us. We'd be plenty safe. But first things first — Brittany needed to be allowed to stay.

"Okay. But remember, you have to call Brittany's mom tonight."

"I will. Just let me get settled."

I hugged Mom hard before Brittany and I went into our own room next door. As typical, Mom and I had adjoining suites with a door in between so we could go back and forth without stepping into the hall.

Fifteen minutes later Brittany and I were in our pajamas, sitting cross-legged on our matching queen beds. Mom hadn't called yet. I'd already dialed her cell phone to say, "Please call Brittany's mother *now*. We're waiting up to hear."

Not that we'd have gone to bed anyway. Brittany and I had passed beyond exhaustion, now too wired to sleep. The chaos of police officers at the Pavilion and the crowds of reporters around our limo had momentarily numbed my pain. In its place — a simmering determination to find justice for Tom.

"I'm going to help the police solve this," I declared.

"Yeah. I'm with you."

Brittany flipped her long hair around and around her right forefinger — a sign she was thinking hard. "Know what? This is a little too convenient — shooting Tom on a night when Rayne isn't performing the next day. Almost like the killer knew he could do it without stopping the tour."

I pursed my lips. That was true. Many times Rayne would have to be in another city for a concert the very next day. With a delay like we'd had tonight, another concert in less than twenty-four hours may not have been possible. "But that makes it sound like someone on the tour did it."

Brittany tilted her head.

"You *think* that, Brittany?"

"I don't know." She lifted both hands. "It's just — Look, why would a local roadie do it? None of them know Tom."

"Maybe the killer *didn't* know him. Maybe the guy was after something in Ross's office, and Tom came in at the wrong time."

"But nothing was taken."

I rubbed the pink silky fabric of my pajama bottoms. "Maybe the guy had to run out before he found what he wanted."

"Like what?"

"I have no idea."

Brittany considered that. "Does Ross carry secret information with him?"

"Depends on what you call secret. You saw those reporters — any one of them would love to know *anything* private about Rayne. Ross's papers include contracts about performance dates. So, yeah, if someone's just dying to know exclusive information, like all the special things Rayne O'Connor insists on having in her dressing room. The blue leather couch, the kinds of food, the size of the mirrors."

"But no reporters could get backstage, right? You told me security guards are everywhere and that only local union workers got in that private back door."

"True. So what if one of those workers wanted the information? He could sell it to a tabloid for a *lot* of money."

Tabloids. I hated them. And their paparazzi.

Flopping back on my bed, I stared at the white ceiling. "It would be such a gamble, carrying around a gun like that. You'd have to stuff it in your pants or something, and what if someone saw it?"

Brittany had no answer.

I sighed. "If Tom was killed only because he saw someone in Ross's office who shouldn't be there, you'd think he'd be just inside the door. Like he stepped into the room to say, 'What are you doing here?' Instead, he was all the way in the room — behind the desk."

"Maybe the killer dragged him there."

I closed my eyes, picturing the carpet. Was it the kind that would show the drag marks of a body? I hadn't seen anything like that.

Brittany's cell phone rang. She checked the ID and winced. "Uh-oh. Home calling."

"Mom probably talked to her."

Despite my trust in Mom's ability to convince, I held my breath as Brittany answered.

"Hi, Mom." Her shoulders tightened, then hunched.

Please, oh please!

Brittany listened.

"Uh-huh. Yeah."

I didn't dare move. Had Mom's call not worked?

Brittany bit her lip. "I know."

My gaze fixed on her face, gauging every expression.

"Remember, Mom," she said. "It happened *here*, in San Jose. And we're leaving on Sunday anyway. Whoever did it must be someone local. So I'll be just as safe going with the tour to Denver as I would if I came home."

I had to hand it to Brittany — she could argue like a lawyer in court. Her mom always said she was destined to be an attorney.

She tensed again, then closed her eyes. "I will. I promise."

I leaned forward.

Brittany's eyes flew open. Her muscles relaxed. She nodded excitedly and gave me a thumbs-up.

My hands raised in the air. *Yes!*

Brittany promised her mother the world. No, she wouldn't go anywhere without a bodyguard. Yes, she'd do everything Rayne O'Connor said. Yes, she'd check in with her worried parents twice a day.

Parents. Unexpectedly, the word bit. A reminder that I had only Mom — and an empty black hole for a father I never knew.

"Okay. Thanks so much! Call you tomorrow." With triumph, Brittany hung up.

"Oh, thank goodness." Weak with relief, I punched in Mom's cell phone number. "Thank you, thank you, thank you. You did it!"

Mom managed a tired chuckle. "I know you need the company. Now you two go to sleep."

"Yeah. Good night."

Some time after three a.m. Brittany and I finally wound down. Yawning, we slid into our beds.

As sleepiness pulsed through my veins, I thought of Tom. My closest friend on tour. Like a big brother. Everyone liked him. Who would want him dead?

Tom, I miss you so much. I will find out who did this to you.

Whoever it was, that person would *pay*.

11

Mom and the band are onstage, performing their last encore song.

After the concert, I peek out from backstage and see my father sitting in the front row. Even though I've never seen him before in my life, have no idea what he looks like — somehow I know.

Breath backs up in my throat.

Everyone else in the arena is leaving, but he claps on, tears of pride in his eyes for Rayne O'Connor. He thrusts a hand up toward her. Suddenly in his fingers — a single white rose wrapped in green cellophane and tied with a red ribbon.

Mom leaves the stage, oblivious.

My heart beats so hard it's about to lift me off the floor. I shuffle onstage, legs trembling. Roadies are breaking down the set around me, but I pay no attention. I only have eyes for my father.

He looks at me, and the wrapped white rose crumbles to nothingness in his hand. Emotions move across his face. Recognition ... shock ... understanding ...

Love.

His arms rise, held up toward me. He moves forward, and so do I. After all the years, I can't believe this is happening. I'm meeting my dad. The missing, vital part of me.

We are twenty feet apart. I am so deliriously happy, I can't even feel my legs moving.

Fifteen feet.

He smiles at me. I smile back.

Ten.

As high as the stage is, somehow I know he'll jump up on it with no problem. Because he wants to with all his heart. Because he won't let anything keep us apart — ever again.

Even my mother.

We are five feet away from each other. His face is a blur through my tears. I hear, "Dad, Dad," and realize it's my own mouth calling him.

Two feet.

His muscles coil to make the huge jump. He bounds into the air like a deer.

The scene jars into slow motion. One of his legs drifts up off the floor, then the other, his hands floating, hair lifting in the breeze. His mouth creaks open, my name forming — Shhhhaaaalllleee ...

His body hangs in the air, rising ... rising ... He is inches away.

Someone yells to his left. His head rotates toward it.

Terror stabs through me. "Daaad," I scream. "Donnn't!"

A shot splits the night. I see the bullet parting air in slow motion, aiming straight for my father. I want to stop it but I can't.

My body turns to ice.

As if in water, my father's limbs struggle to change course.

It's ... too ... late ...

The bullet slams him in the left eye.

His head turns toward me for one last look. I see the black of his empty socket, his right eye shining with love for me.

Light fades from that eye. Fades ... fades.

It flattens in death.

He sinks to the floor and out of my sight.

Grief cuts me in two. "Nooo!" I wail. "No, no ..."

A rattled scream in my throat jerked me awake.

My heart raced, and sweat coated my forehead. For a moment I couldn't even *think*. I stared up at the ceiling, fighting to see something, anything. With the heavy curtains closed, the hotel room was nearly pitch dark.

I could hear Brittany breathing as she slept.

My body wouldn't stop shaking.

Just a dream, I tried to tell myself. *Just a dream.*

But it felt so real. My father seemed *so real.*

No matter how many times I've begged, my mom refuses to tell me who he is. Someone she dated in high school is all she'll say. Someone she loved very much. Who gave her single white roses wrapped in green cellophane and tied with a red ribbon as a symbol of his love. By the time she was seventeen and gave birth to me, he was out of her life. He can't even know for sure that he's my father, she insists.

The dream echoed in my mind. I wanted it back. I wanted to see my father again.

It isn't fair for Mom to keep him from me.

"How can he not know about me?" I've asked many times. "Didn't he see you pregnant?"

When she learned about the pregnancy, he was already gone, she says — always with lowered eyes and pain in her face.

"Do you know where he is now?"

"No."

The answer never changes. Still I ask. Because I don't believe her. I think she does know. I think she doesn't want to tell me.

What is she protecting me from?

A moan slipped from my mouth. I didn't want to wake Brittany. I rolled on my side away from her, buried my face in the pillow, and cried. For Tom, the friend I had lost that day, and for the father I had never known. And then, irrationally, but terrifying all the same, for what I might lose tomorrow.

PART 2
Saturday

12

I woke slowly, fighting the day. Fresh grief over Tom weighted me to the bed. How I wished his death had been only another nightmare.

By the time Brittany and I got up, it was past eleven. I felt almost drugged, like I hadn't slept at all.

Brittany cocked her head and surveyed me. "What's wrong? I mean, something new."

I rubbed my face. "I had a dream."

"About what?"

The scene rushed over me, trailing all the emotions. My father's face. His love. The white rose. The gunshot. I focused on the floor. "My father."

"Oh."

Maybe it was the violent loss of Tom. Or my determination to help solve his murder. Whatever it was, at that moment I no longer merely resented the fact that Mom wouldn't tell me about my father. I *hated* it.

And I was old enough to do something about it.

I gave Brittany a wry smile and shrugged. "You hungry?"

"Yeah."

We ordered room service — two personal pizzas and salads.

I hung up the phone and turned on the TV, flipping to a cable news station.

Tom's face filled the screen, followed by footage of our limo, surrounded by reporters, driving from the arena parking lot.

"Oh!" Brittany drew to the TV like a magnet.

Clutching our arms we listened to the reporter's story.

Behind the darkly tinted glass of the limo, our faces were dim. I caught a glimpse of my own features, Brittany's ducked head.

"Great." she mumbled. "Mom's gonna see this."

I searched the faces of the crowd around our car but saw no paparazzi member I recognized. Their features were too blurred, the bodies in motion too chaotic.

The reporter turned to an interview of a San Jose policeman who'd been on scene. The officer disclosed very little. Nothing I didn't already know.

The picture switched to a commercial. I changed channels, and we watched last night's limo scene all over again from a slightly different camera angle.

"Why don't they talk about *Tom*?" I cried. "So *what* if Rayne and Shaley O'Connor are in that limo. Tom's *dead!*"

Furiously, I punched in a new channel. News show after news show — the same thing. Tom's picture and murder were overshadowed by reporters and talking heads stating opinions about what this might mean for Rayne and their tour.

I smacked off the TV. "They make me sick."

Blurry-eyed, I paced the room, arms folded. "I swear if any reporter shoves a microphone in my face and asks about Tom like he's no more than a dramatic entertainment story, I'll knock that person flat. They don't deserve to even *speak* Tom's name."

Brittany sank dejectedly onto her bed. "So … now what? Do we just stay in the room all day?"

I pulled to a halt. "No way. We're going shopping, *just* like we planned."

"Oh. But your mom said — "

"I know what she said. But can you imagine if we don't go. We'll have nothing to do but sit around this room all day. And *think*." New tears burned my eyes. I couldn't sit around thinking about Tom all day. It hurt too much.

Brittany looked dubious. "Will your mom let us go?"

"We'll just have to persuade her. Let's get dressed and all ready to go. Then it'll be harder for her to stop us. You know, like in business — assume the sale."

Truth was I would be playing on Mom's weakness. Ever since Rayne rocketed to stardom she had far less time for me. Now what she couldn't give me in personal attention, she tried to make up for in money and leniency.

Brittany mushed her lips and nodded. "Okay."

We got dressed and put on our makeup, stopping to eat our pizzas and salads when they arrived. Sometime later, we knocked on the door connecting our room to Mom's room.

It opened to reveal Mom in her silk charmeuse loungewear, no makeup. She gave us both a long look. "You two girls look mighty fancy to stay in your rooms today."

I shot Brittany a look. "You know we're not staying in our room. You promised us weeks ago we could go shopping."

Mom's eyelids flickered. "That was before Tom ... died."

I looked down at my feet and sighed. Part of me knew how shallow it sounded — fighting to go shopping a day after one of my good friends was killed. The other part reminded me it was either keep busy or go crazy with remembering. "Do you really want us to sit around and do nothing all day? You've got a photo shoot and interview in a couple of hours. It'll take your mind off this — at least for awhile. We need something too."

Mom shook her head. "Have you turned on the TV? They're all over the story, as we expected."

A chill blew over me. "We saw it."

"So I can't let you go out in this circus atmosphere."

"I'll go in disguise. They'll never know it's me."

"And if that doesn't work?"

"It will."

We surveyed each other. I could tell Mom was caving. She knew

what I'd been through yesterday. She knew I craved some semblance of my normal life back.

If you could call our lives "normal."

"Come on, Mom. We'll have a bodyguard with us. Two if you
like. And if something happens, we'll hop in the limo and leave
right away."

Mom's gaze turned to Brittany. "You sure you want to do this?
You got a little taste last night of how it can be if things get out of
hand."

Brittany nodded. "I know. But we've been looking forward to
this for weeks. And Shaley especially—I think she needs to get out."

I suppressed a smile. Brittany knew how to play Mom as well
as I did.

Someone knocked on the room's hall door. "Oh, that's Marshall."
Mom glanced toward it, suddenly all business. "Look, I have to get
ready. Go—and take Bruce. Wendell and Mick are with me today.
Shaley, keep your disguise on. And *do not* stray out of Bruce's sight."

Brittany and I threw each other triumphant glances. "I will,
Mom, don't worry. Have a good interview!"

"Thanks, Rayne!" Brittany grinned.

"Yeah, yeah. I hope I'm not sorry later."

Brittany and I backed into our room and closed the connecting
door before Mom could change her mind.

"Whew." Brittany flipped bangs out of her eyes. "That was
close."

I dug in my purse for the code list to call Bruce's room. Now that
freedom was near, we couldn't leave soon enough. I wanted *away*
from those four walls of bad dreams about my father and thoughts
of Tom.

As I reached for the receiver, the phone rang. I picked it up,
distracted. "Hello." My eyes flicked from my suitcase to Brittany. I
covered the receiver's mouthpiece. "Would you get my short black
wig out of there?"

Brittany moved to the suitcase. Someone—sounded like a
young woman—was talking into the phone.

"I'm sorry, what?"

"This is the front desk, Miss O'Connor. Sorry to bother you, but someone left a gift for you here."

A gift?

Some Rayne fan must have found our hotel. Wouldn't be the first time. They usually left things for Mom, but after all the publicity photos I'd appeared in with her in the last couple years, now people followed me around too. Last year some older man kept leaving me "presents." Photos of himself without a lot of clothes on. We turned them over to the police. The man stopped bothering me.

Rayne does have many wonderful fans, but unfortunately there are a lot of weirdos out there.

I watched Brittany pull out the wig and shake it. Ugly thing.

"Would you like me to send it up?" the desk clerk asked.

Brittany handed the wig to me. I took it, making a face. "Uh, sure, whatever. But do it now because we're about to leave."

"All right. It'll be there in a minute."

I clicked off the line, then pushed *talk* again to phone Bruce. He said he'd call for a car right away. "Thanks so much!" I threw down the phone and positioned myself in front of the mirror, sighing. "I wish I didn't have to do this."

"*Freedom*, Shaley. That wig spells freedom."

Brittany and her lawyer logic.

I stuffed my long hair under the wig and moved the thing around until it looked right.

A knock sounded. "Want to check the peephole, Brittany? It's probably a bellman with that gift."

She moved to the door. "Yeah, it's him."

"Okay, open up. I'll get him a tip." I snatched my wallet from my purse and pulled out a five. At the door I thrust the bill into the bellman's hands and accepted a long white box. "Thanks for bringing it."

"You're welcome, Miss. And thank *you*."

Brittany shut the door and bolted it. "Looks like something from a florist."

"Yeah. Let's hope it's nothing weird."

I sat on the edge of her bed and studied the box. No florist name on it anywhere.

Maybe it would be on a card inside.

Like the settling of a fitful breeze, all my swirling anticipation to get out of the room and go shopping abruptly died away. Tom's face blazed into my mind. His one open eye, the other blown apart.

His killer was still out there.

I should have questioned the girl at the front desk about who had brought this package.

Brittany sidled over to stand beside me. "You going to open it?"

I pulled my lip between my teeth and stared at the box. Ran a finger over its smoothness. "I don't know. After yesterday ..."

Silence.

Brittany swallowed. "It's probably just flowers."

"I know but ... Do you feel something? Anything?"

"No."

Not that this meant anything. Brittany's weird ability to sense things showed up when it pleased.

I took a deep breath. "What should I do?"

"Open it. You have to know. If it's something bad, we'll call the police."

It won't be anything bad, I chided myself. I was just being paranoid.

All the same, the back of my neck started to tingle.

"Okay." My muscles tensed. "Here goes."

Carefully I laid the box on the bed beside me. I placed my fingers on both sides of the top and lifted it away.

I gazed at the contents. My heart stopped.

My mouth dropped open, the tingles at my neck now like stinging ants. All breath bottled up in my throat.

In the box — a single white rose, wrapped in green cellophane and tied with a red ribbon.

13

He had been born superior to others.

At the tender age of five, he knew that already. In kindergarten, he was smarter. In elementary school, more cunning. Other kids cried when they got hurt or because they didn't want to leave their mothers dropping them off at school. *He* never did. His intellect was too strong for that. Emotions were secondary.

Now, thirteen hours after he'd had to kill, he celebrated his success as he ate a roast beef and cheese sandwich for lunch. The police had questioned him twice last night — along with everyone else — but with so many people around, so many possible suspects on the tour and working locally, the interview had been less than thorough. Within two minutes he'd outwitted the slow detective.

They found the gun, of course. He knew they would. It could never be traced to him. They had not found the elbow-length glove he'd worn when he pulled the trigger. He knew all about blowback — microscopic particles emitted from a gun when it was fired. Just in case the police decided to test the hands of everyone in the vicinity for gun residue, he'd slipped on the glove before the murder, then thrown it underneath a row of seats on the arena's first tier after the encore. With all the fans milling around, no one noticed, and he knew the arena would soon be cleaned while the police concentrated on containing the backstage area.

The job was done. It had taken far too many days to plan. Still, when the timing was right, it was brilliantly executed. Naturally.

But deep within him, jealousy burned on.

He took another huge bite of his sandwich. A swig of Coke.

For a while he had denied the jealousy, or at least tried to call it by another name. How could a man as superior as he be weighted down by such an inferior emotion? As time passed and the feeling grew stronger, he realized what an asset it could be. Emotions aren't weak in themselves; it's all in how they're handled. He would stoke the fire of his jealousy, keep it burning bright, as he protected the Special One.

He finished the sandwich and wiped his mouth and fingers with a napkin. Then he laced his hands and cracked every knuckle. How good it sounded, the popping of his bones. Made him feel so *alive*.

A yawn sagged his mouth open. Last night's adrenaline rush had afforded him little sleep. But no time to rest now.

He had duties to perform.

14

Brittany stood over me, fingers to her mouth, staring at the rose. My hands hovered above the box, unable to draw back, fearful to touch the flower lest it crumble away like the one in my dream.

Mom, myself, Brittany. We were the *only* ones who knew the significance of this gift. Other than my father.

I stared at the box, my vision blurring.

"Isn't that a card?" Brittany whispered. "Underneath."

Could this *really* be ...? "He's not supposed to even know who I am."

"I know."

Slowly my trembling fingers reached inside the box. I touched the soft velvet of the petals, heard the crinkle of cellophane as I reached beneath for the card and pulled it out.

Across the front in hand-printed letters: SHALEY. "Preston Floral" read the business name on the envelope.

I pressed my fingertips to the printed letters. Had my father written them? Was I now touching something he had touched?

Holding my breath, I slid my finger underneath the flap.

All the times I'd wished for my father, all the tears I'd shed. My daydreams never told the story this way. In my fanciful wishing he always showed up in the flesh, magically walking into my life as if he'd never left it. Never to leave again.

The envelope slit across the top. I reached inside for the card. It was folded over, white, with a calligraphy *S* on the front.

Throat tightening, I opened it.

Shaley,

I'm watching over you.

I read the words five times.

What *was* this? Why would my father write such a message?

Brittany leaned over to see, and I tilted the card toward her. She spoke the message aloud.

"You think that's your dad?"

"I don't know."

She sat down on the bed. "Doesn't it have to be? No one but your mom knows about the white rose."

My fingers rubbed the smooth card. "Maybe it's just a coincidence."

"Some coincidence. I mean, just a white rose, maybe. But the green cellophane *and* a red ribbon —"

"Why wouldn't he say so then? Why this vague message?" I swallowed. "I'm not even sure I like what it says."

Brittany's eyes lowered to the card. "I know. After what happened last night, it's almost kind of ... creepy."

I stared at the rose. "If Mom saw this, she'd freak."

"You going to tell her?"

I shook my head. "Not now. Tom's death is upsetting enough. She's interviewing this afternoon, and tomorrow we have to travel. Then she performs again tomorrow night. Why lay this on her?"

"But maybe she'd have some idea who sent it if it wasn't your dad."

"Oh, she'd *insist* it wasn't him." My voice edged. "He's not supposed to know I exist, remember?"

Truth was, I didn't want Mom to crush my hope. Even if the note did feel kind of creepy, it wasn't meant to be, I told myself. Not at all. My father had sent it, and when he was ready, he'd tell me his name. He'd arrange to meet me.

Please, God.

"I need to find out about the person who brought this."

I put the card down and walked over to the phone. Punched 0 for the front desk.

"Yes, Miss O'Connor."

It was the woman who'd called me. I recognized her voice.

"Hi. I just wanted to ask about the person who left this rose for me. Did you see him?"

"A cab driver brought it."

"A *cab driver*?"

Brittany twisted her mouth.

"Yes. He just said it was a delivery. He put it on the counter and left."

My heart sank. "Oh. Okay. Thank you."

I clicked off the line.

Disappointment rippled through me. The note could still be from my dad. But if so, he obviously didn't want me to find him. Delivery by a cab driver. How impersonal could you get?

I glared at the phone, then pushed *talk* to dial outside the hotel for 4 – 1 – 1. "What's the name of the florist, Brittany?"

She picked up the envelope. "Preston Floral."

From the operator I got the number and punched it in. My pulse snagged as I listened to the line ring. Did I really want to find out who'd sent the rose? As long as I didn't know, I could hope — "

"Good afternoon, Preston Floral." A cheery woman's voice.

"Hello. My name is Shaley O'Connor. I just received a beautiful white rose sent by cab from your shop. Could you tell me anything about the person who bought it from you?"

I glanced nervously at Brittany. She stood nearby, arms clutched, watching my face.

"Yes, Miss O'Connor. I'm glad you like the rose. But the purchaser didn't come into the shop. It was ordered over the phone."

My shoulders slumped. *On the phone*, I mouthed to Brittany. "Was it a man's voice?"

"Yes, I took the order myself."

"How'd he pay for it?"

"By credit card."

"Then you must have a name for the card."

"Oh, goodness, with all the orders we get, I couldn't possibly remember. This is a big shop. Besides — "

"Can't you look it up?"

"As I was about to say, we have a store policy against giving out that information."

"*Please.* It's really important."

"I can't, really."

"But you *have* to. I *need* to know."

"I'm sorry. I cannot break store policy."

Heat flushed my cheeks. "Just this once can't hurt."

"Miss O'Connor." Her voice firmed. "I *cannot* give you that information."

I knew the tone. She thought I was being a brat just because of who I was. *Shaley O'Connor thinks she can get anything she wants because she's the spoiled rich daughter of a rock star.* Normally I would have cared. Normally I would have bent over backward to be nice.

"Great. Thanks for nothing." I punched off the line and slammed down the phone.

Anger and fear sloshed around inside me. I balled up my hands, tears biting my eyes.

"Shaley, I'm sorry," Brittany said.

"Yeah, me too." Pain over my father mixed with grief about Tom. What was *happening* in my life? Why all this stuff at once?

And if my father sent the rose, *why* would he want to torture me like this?

With a small cry I stalked to the bed, snatched up the card, and stuffed it back beneath the rose. I clamped on the box's lid, threw the thing in my suitcase, and closed the top.

There. Now I didn't have to look at it.

The phone rang. My head jerked toward it, all anger whisking into sodden hope. Was it the woman, changing her mind?

I picked up the phone, my hands jittery. "Hello?"

"Hi." Bruce's deep Lurch voice. "The car's out front. You two ready?"

I let out a long breath. "Oh." Shopping. I'd forgotten all about it. "Yeah."

"All right. I'll be at your door in thirty seconds."

Brittany and I sat on one seat in the small limo, facing Bruce on the other. I was still half numb. The driver had recommended going to the Valley Fair Mall — a large shopping center not too far from our hotel.

"Great," I said. "Whatever."

Bruce shot me a searching look. I turned away and looked out the window.

The driver dropped us off in front of a main entrance and said he would park under the shade of the buildings to wait for us. When we called, he'd return to that entrance within minutes.

"Hope you have a book to read." I slid from the limo as the driver held open the door. "We'll probably be awhile."

He shrugged. "That's what you hired me for."

At the door to the mall I took a deep breath. Thoughts of Tom and the white rose pulsed in my head. I craved distraction. I wanted those thoughts *out* of my brain.

"Brittany, we're going to have a good time, right?"

She nodded firmly. "Right."

Inside the mall we stopped at an information map, checking out store locations. I ran my finger down the list of women's stores. Near the top — Abercrombie and Fitch.

Brittany grinned. "Let's go."

The mall was crowded. We wove through shoppers, Bruce on my right and Brittany on my left. Every now and then Bruce would slowly run his thumb and fingers down his goatee — a habit that made him look even more formidable. Anyone who noticed our trio was eyeing him, not me in my black wig. Bruce was hard to miss.

Brittany's cell phone kept going off. Mine too. The calls were from friends at home who'd heard the news, asking if we were okay. And pumping us for information. The very thing we came to forget for a while, we couldn't seem to get away from. We answered the questions quickly — *yeah, we're okay, thanks for checking* — and said we had to go. Brittany's mom called too.

"Yes, Mom, we're fine," Brittany told her. "We're shopping and being guarded by the *biggest* guy you ever saw in your life."

Bruce heard but didn't crack a smile. His eyes roamed the wide mall, watching people. Sometimes I think he has a computer for a brain, and every face he sees goes into a data file.

We bought a couple of shirts at Abercrombie. The hot guy behind the counter (they're *always* hot at that store) flicked a look at me when he saw the name on my credit card. I was prepared to give my typical disclaimer response — *oh, yeah, I share the name of a famous person* — but he said nothing.

All the same, when we left that store, I threw a look back at him. The guy was on his cell phone, staring at me. He blinked away.

"Something wrong?" Bruce didn't break stride, but I saw the tension in his muscles.

I hesitated. So what if the clerk recognized me? He hadn't made a scene.

"Guess not."

I didn't dare look back again. Apprehension hovered about me like a cold fog. The way that sales guy looked at me while he was on the phone ...

No. We were here to have fun. I *would not* think about it.

Brittany and I headed for the Savvy section in Nordstrom.

We ended up trying on one pair of designer jeans after another, plus a whole stack of tops. For every piece of clothing, we checked each other with a critical eye. Only pure honesty works when we're shopping. No point in saying something looks great if it doesn't.

"The color's perfect for you."

"Those jeans make you look really skinny."

"Well, it's just *okay*."

"Uh-uh. That shirt looks better on the hanger."

Bruce hung around outside the dressing room, probably scaring half the customers to death. More than once I heard his deep voice say to some inquiring sales person, "I'm just waiting for two girls in there. They're trying on every piece of clothing in the place."

I told Brittany I'd buy her whatever she wanted. Mom's accountant would take care of paying my monthly credit card bill without even blinking. Mom never cared how much I spent.

We didn't exactly buy out the store, but we did get three pairs of designer jeans each, plus a total of fifteen tops. Bruce offered to carry the bags (he already held the one from Abercrombie), but we said, "No thanks." It wasn't really fair to make him lug around all that stuff. I shoved my purse on my shoulder and took two bags, giving Brittany the third.

Bruce stroked his beard, then made a point of looking at his watch as we walked away from the cash register. "You two done yet? You've worn me out."

Brittany made a *tsss* sound. "Worn *you* out? *We're* the ones who had to try on everything." She gave him a look, trying to coax a smile out of him. He just flicked his eyes at the ceiling and sighed.

"Where to next?" I asked as we crossed out of Nordstrom into the busy mall.

That's when I heard my name called — and saw the first flash go off.

16

At the sound of my name, my head automatically turned. Too late I realized my terrible mistake.

Vulture.

I recognized the face at once. Mom and I had given him the nickname. Ed Whisk, a tall, gangly man with extra skin on his neck and beady eyes. He works for that lying, down-in-the-dirt tabloid *Shock.*

"Found you, Shaley." He smiled, showing yellow teeth, and clicked his camera.

I gasped and stopped in my tracks. Brittany grabbed my arm.

"It's okay, girls," Bruce said in a low voice. "Just keep walking. We'll head for the nearest exit."

From all points, more photographers descended. Someone had tipped them off. One camera became two, three ... five ... six ... I knew over half the faces. Frog, the ugly woman with the wide mouth and googly green eyes, who's with the tabloid *All That's Hot.* And Cat, a gangly, effeminate man with bleached white-blond hair and two inches of black roots, working for *Cashing In.* Plus two freelancers we called Frodo and Gollum, after the characters in *Lord of the Rings.*

I pictured the Abercrombie clerk on his cell phone and wanted to strangle him.

It would only take one call to bring these people running. They'd probably all flocked to San Jose as soon as the news about

Tom's death broke. Once one of them discovered our trail, the others had followed like hounds.

My heart tripped over itself. Being caught among a crowd in a limo was bad enough. But exposed like this — so open and vulnerable — I felt absolutely crushed.

The exit seemed a million miles away.

"Hey, Shaley, love the wig!" A photographer I didn't recognize darted close to me like some mosquito. He gave me a smarmy grin. The man was short and skinny with wild brown hair and deep-set, coal-black eyes. His nose wrinkled as he clicked his camera again and again.

Brittany held tighter to my arm. Carrying two bags, I didn't have an extra hand to shield my face. I turned my head this way and that, but every time found myself staring into a camera.

At the commotion, shoppers looked around and exchanged comments. I heard the words *black hair* followed by *wig* as people saw past my disguise. A young couple ran toward me. Two girls. Three guys. Five more girls. Women and men and kids — like an avalanche picking up speed, rolling toward us.

"Shaleeeeey." Brittany pressed against me, her eyes wide.

In seconds, they swarmed over us.

"Get back!" Bruce shouted. He moved in front of us, right hand up, palm out. "Let us through." He pushed forward, parting people like a gunboat through water, the two of us in his wake.

The crowd pressed in tighter, hands reaching to touch me and trying to snatch off my wig. I thrust both bags into one hand, ducking down to cover my head with the other arm. Feet stepped on mine, people jostling me and calling my name. Someone pushed into me, and I stumbled to one side. Brittany and I screamed. *No, don't fall!* If I went down I'd be trampled.

Bruce turned and caught my arm in an iron vise. He pulled me up straight. "Hold onto me. Keep moving."

Shoppers thrust cell phones in my face, snapping pictures. Others shouted into their phones, "Get over here right now. Shaley

O'Connor's here!" More and more people rushed over, the paparazzi cursing and shoving.

My mouth hung open, dragging in air. All these people around me, sucking up oxygen. I couldn't *breathe.*

New voices yelled my name, the shouts ricocheting throughout the mall. Reporters materialized with microphones. "Shaley, is it true you found Tom Hutchens's body?"

Flash.

"Did you see his blown-out eye?"

Flash, flash.

"Who do you think killed him?"

Flash.

"Was he a good friend of yours?"

Bruce yelled in their faces and pushed them away. It did no good. As big as he was, he was outnumbered by a hundred. The crowd swarmed in tighter. I could hear Brittany crying behind me. I tipped my head up toward the ceiling, desperate for air.

A dozen flashes went off.

Bruce's hands rose. Cat shoved in beneath one of his arms and stuck his camera in my face. The flash nearly blinded me. I cried out and ducked my head back down.

"Get outta here!" Bruce surged between Cat and me. One of his hands fumbled to pull out his cell phone. I knew he was trying to call the limo driver. If he dropped the phone, he'd never be able to get down and pick it up.

"Shaley," a reporter called, "what did Tom look like when you found him?"

Something hit the base of my neck. The wig knocked down on my forehead, half covering my eyes. I shoved it back.

"Where was he?"

"Is the Rayne tour going to continue?"

"Shaley, come on! What do you know?"

Tears bit my eyes. "*Stop* it! Leave me *alone!*"

Camera flashes pummeled me. I covered my face.

Dimly, I heard Bruce shouting into his phone for the limo.

"Shaley, how well did you know Tom?"

"How do you *feel* about the murder?"

Panic and anger and fear gnawed at my chest. My legs weakened. I wasn't going to make it. Any second now I'd fall.

A new bright light poured over me. I swung around to see a TV camera. A female reporter shoved a microphone at me. "Shaley, do you think the killer is part of your tour group?"

"No!" Tears spilled down my cheeks. "Go away!"

"Hey, hey, get back!" Two mall security guards rushed to the crowd, trying to help.

Through blurred vision, I saw the exit in the distance.

Bruce pulled us up in front of him, me on one side of his chest, Brittany on the other. He wrapped his huge arms around us. "Move toward the door!" he shouted in our ears.

Inch by inch we battled our way, jostled on every side. The mall security guards fought past crushing bodies and cameras and arms and legs to reach us and form a front barrier.

"Shaley, tell us about Tom!"

"What did his face look like?"

"Where's Rayne? How does she feel about the murder?"

After an eternity, we reached the exit.

The mall guards pushed through a door, holding it open for the three of us. As we passed through, they wedged in behind us. The limo waited nearby, back door ajar. I threw myself inside, sliding over my bags and ending up on the floor. Brittany came right behind me, followed by Bruce. He slammed the door shut and locked it.

The limo took off.

Breathing hard and crying, I nudged myself up on the seat next to Brittany. We clung to each other. Bruce collapsed on the seat opposite us, facing backward. His cheeks were beet red, a thick vein pulsing in his forehead.

Bruce surged forward on his seat, craning his neck to check through windows on both sides and the back. "No one's following.

Yet." He swiveled to push back the small sliding door in the barrier
between us and the driver. "How far to the freeway?"

"Real close, sir."

"When you get on it, take the first exit, and do some double-
backs on surface streets. We can't have anyone follow us to the
hotel."

"Yes, sir."

Bruce huffed back in his seat, facing me and Brittany. Seeing our tears, he snatched two tissues from a built-in holder and
pressed them into our hands. "Sorry, Shaley." His voice was low,
eyes narrowed. He looked like he wanted to punch a hole in somebody's face.

"You don't have to apologize." I hiccupped, wiping at my face.
"You got us out of there."

He made a sound in his throat. "Barely. Good thing the mall
guards came along."

Brittany clutched her tissue. "All those *people*. I just can't believe
how fast they came." She shuddered.

One of the shopping bags sat half on my foot. I kicked it off.
"I *hate* that Vulture. And Frog, and Cat, and all the rest of them."

Brittany made a face. "Wasn't it Vulture's tabloid that said your
mom found you in a dumpster when you were a baby?"

"Yeah. *Shock*. They're also the ones that ran that fake story
about Mom's wild sex parties. Vulture's the one that took the pictures of the outside of our house and of us coming and going. He
camped out on our street for days."

"Your mom should sue them for lying. *You* should sue them all
for what they just did."

"It's too hard." My words were bitter. "We're famous people."

"So?"

"So the courts have hard standards for proving lies if you're famous. We don't have the time or energy."

"That's not *fair*."

I gave Brittany a humorless smile. "Yeah, I know. Welcome to the Rayne tour."

She shook her head and glared out the window.

My tears had stopped, but my limbs still shook. I leaned forward, elbows on my knees, and gazed unseeing into the shopping bag nearest my feet. The reporters' questions battered my head.

Didn't you find Tom? What did his face look like? Do you think someone on tour killed him?

Anger rippled through me. I wanted to tear every one of those people apart.

A dark rectangular shape in the shopping bag punched into my consciousness.

I blinked, stared at it.

A photo?

Where had that come from?

Slowly, as if it could bite, I reached into the bag and drew it out.

It was a picture of me from last night — getting out of the limo in the hotel parking lot.

My mouth hinged open. Who could have taken this? We hadn't seen *anyone*. And why had it been put in my shopping bag?

Somehow, I knew there was more. My fingers flipped the picture over.

On the back, in block red letters — the words that chilled me to the core.

Always Watching.

17

How disgusting, he thought, *the way Tom Hutchens's murder plasters the news.* The man had been worth nothing in life. Why now so important in death?

Regardless of where they were right now, he knew every person on the tour would see the coverage. The main entourage staying in the San Jose hotel had much of the day free. The stage manager and roadies on the way to Denver could watch the small satellite TVs on the specially outfitted bus.

What a frustrating day — with the tour members split up. No way to keep his eye on everyone. If only he could be two places at once.

As superior as he was to the rest of humanity, even *he* could not manage that.

Tomorrow they would all be reunited.

A second death could wreak havoc with the tour. That was not his intent. Nor was it in his own best interest. If other killings became necessary, his best approach would be to make them appear as accidents.

The world was indeed a savage place. Accidents occurred every day.

When he was five, he'd witnessed the freak incident that took his own father's life. They were in the workshop area of the garage, his father wielding a buzz saw against a plank of wood. The saw hit an unseen nail and jarred. In a split second it jumped out of the cut line and shot straight toward his father's left arm.

The deadly blade sliced through just above the elbow.

Blood flew in all directions. Spattered on his own upturned face. His father dropped the saw as the severed limb bounced against the wall and fell. The blade stopped whirring.

He couldn't move. Couldn't scream. Could only stare as his father sank to both knees, then collapsed on the cold concrete.

His mother was out running errands. He knew he should get to the phone, call 9 – 1 – 1. At five, he was already intelligent enough to do that. But as he gawked at his father's unconscious form, disappointment stirred within him. What a *stupid* accident. How could his own father do something so dumb?

Still, he had to save him.

He glanced toward the door — the one that led into the kitchen and the life-saving phone — and cold panic overtook him. His body turned to lead. Try as he might, he couldn't move his legs.

Helplessly, he watched his father bleed to death.

When the garage door opened to his mother's car, he melted into a puddle of shaking and tears.

Days later when he cried to her about his guilt, she told him it wasn't his fault. But he could never forgive himself. As he grew he could only harden his own spirit to keep from *feeling*. He'd pushed the memory into a corner of his head, far away from his heart.

Yes, he thought now. Accidents happened. Bloody, deadly, horrific accidents. Many times they were no one's fault.

But the time might come when he had to help one along.

ook." I shoved the picture into Brittany's hands. She looked at it, front and back, and gasped.

"Let me see that." Bruce leaned forward, arm stretched out. Brittany thrust the photo at him as if it burned her fingers.

He examined the picture, then the words on the back.

Brittany and I looked at each other. No one else knew I'd already received another, similar message that morning on a card along with a white rose, and not seeming nearly so threatening. Even if it had hit me as a little creepy, I could have argued it was harmless. I so wanted to believe my father had sent it.

Until now.

Two "watching" messages within hours of each other. And those within a day of Tom's murder. Was the same person behind all this?

Bruce dropped the photo back in my shopping bag. "You need to show that to the police. Looks like some kind of stalker."

Bruce worked for my mom, not me. He would tell her as soon as possible. No way could I keep this from her.

My cell phone rang. I fished it from my purse and checked caller ID. *Mom.*

What timing.

Flipping open the phone, I worked to steady my voice. No need to upset her right now. She'd hear soon enough.

"Hi, Mom. Aren't you in your interview?"

"Just finished." Mom used her clipped business tone. "I'm

headed back to the hotel. Just got a call from Detective Furlow. He wants to meet with you now, ask you some more questions."

Dread filtered through me. All I wanted to do was get back to my room and hide from the world. "Why?"

"Evidently they've found some new information they need to ask you about."

"What?"

"I don't know. We'll hear soon. I'm not letting them talk to you without my being there."

The white rose. My eyes closed, and I leaned my head against the seat. I'd have to tell Mom. Because I'd have to tell the detective about its message and now the photo in my bag.

"How far are you from the hotel?" she asked.

"Close."

"Good. We'll meet with the detective in my room."

"Okay." I bit my lip. "Before the detective comes, I need to talk to you." I wasn't about to show him the white rose without telling her about it first.

"Okay." She sounded distracted. "We're pulling into the hotel. See you soon."

She clicked off the line.

I held the dead phone to my ear, Mom's words trailing through my mind. *New information they need to ask you about.*

The way things had been going, it couldn't be good.

When we reached the hotel, Bruce escorted Brittany and me up to our room. I still felt a little trembly. We carried our shopping bags inside and set them down. The photo glared up at me.

Bruce checked in the bathroom and closet. "Make sure you put on the extra bolt." He gestured toward the door.

"Don't worry."

He headed out.

"Bruce?"

"Yeah."

"Thanks again."

He ran a hand down his goatee and gave me something close to a smile. "No problem."

"I'm going to give that picture to the detective. He might want to talk to you about what happened."

"He knows where to find me."

When he stepped into the hall, I closed and bolted the door.

Tiredness flowed through me as I walked to my bed and sank down on the edge of the mattress. I narrowed my eyes at my suitcase. The white rose was in there. Probably withered by now.

"You'd better go so you have time to talk to your mom before the detective gets here." Brittany sounded tense. She lifted her new jeans from a bag. "I'll take everything out for you. Cut off the tags."

Nervous energy. She was trying to keep busy. "Thanks."

Wincing, she plucked the "always watching" photo from a second bag and laid it on top of the TV. "Here."

With a sigh, I pushed to my feet and headed for the bathroom to fix my tear-tracked makeup. One look at my face like this, and Mom would guess what we'd been through.

Done with that, I changed into one of my new pairs of designer jeans and a pink top. I checked myself in front of the full-length mirror.

"Looks good." Brittany had laid all her new clothes on the bed. "Shaley, thanks again for these."

"Sure." Both of us were trying to sound excited about the clothes, but our hearts weren't in it anymore. We'd have done better to stay in the room and watch movies all day.

I crossed the room to my suitcase, peeled back the lid and picked up the boxed rose. It still looked fresh. "You hungry?"

"No."

"Me either."

Facing Brittany, I took a deep breath. I knew what was going to happen. As much as I would try to hold back, I could feel the old questions rattling around in me already. No way could my Mom and I talk about a white rose without mentioning my dad. And those conversations, full of questions that refused to be answered, never went well.

One look at me, and Brittany knew my thoughts. She walked over and gave me a hug. "It'll be fine. You'll see."

I nodded.

The "always watching" picture — my second problem — still lay on the TV. If I approached Mom with it in my hand, she'd want to know what it was right away.

I picked up the photo and stuck it in my purse.

Here goes.

Holding the boxed rose down against my leg, purse on my shoulder, I knocked on the connecting door that led to Mom's room.

The latch clicked. Mom swung the door open.

"Hi, honey."

"Hi."

She'd changed into jeans and a casual button shirt but was still in all her makeup from the interview and photo shoot. She looked fantastic. Marshall had done her eyes dramatically in mauve, gray, and dark blue with glitter in the eyeliner. Perfectly applied blusher accented her high cheekbones.

Pain stabbed me, and I glanced away. Tom hadn't been dead twenty-four hours, and already Marshall was taking over. Like we didn't need Tom at all. I knew it was irrational, but at that moment I resented everything about Marshall. I'd always liked him before. But now just picturing him — his wide jowls, the black dreadlocked hair, and diamond studs in his ears — I felt resentment racing through my veins.

I forced my eyes back to Mom. "You look so pretty." If only Tom had done her makeup, she'd look even better.

Mom smiled, and little tired lines appeared around her eyes. "Thanks." She gave me a sad look, as if she'd read my thoughts. "I miss him too."

I pressed my lips together and nodded.

Mom cleared her throat. "That outfit new?"

"Yeah. Like it?" My voice sounded dull. But I turned around, giving her full view of the jeans and top.

"Yes. Looks good on you."

I shut the door, leaving it unlocked. We walked over to swiveling gold armchairs in the lounge area and sat down. I put my purse on the floor. "How was the interview and photo shoot?"

"Ill timed." She sighed. "The photo shoot was fine, but all the interviewer wanted to talk about was last night's murder. She thought she'd stumbled onto a gold mine, talking to me so exclusively after the story broke." Mom tossed back her hair. "How was shopping?"

I licked my lips. Juvenile as it sounded, I didn't want to admit to Mom she'd been right. "It ... didn't work. Paparazzi and reporters came. We had to shove our way out."

"Oh, Shaley." Her eyes rounded. "I know how much those crowds scare you."

I shrugged. "It was okay. We managed."

She looked at me askance. "I should never have let you go."

My gaze slid to the floor.

"No wonder I didn't see any paparazzi." Guilt etched Mom's voice. "They were all following *you*."

"It's okay. Really." I gave her a smile. It came out crooked.

She sighed. "Getting to the airport tomorrow might be a zoo too. All those folks could be waiting for us."

Oh, joy. "Once we're through security, it'll be okay."

We were silent for a moment. I knew my feigned optimism wasn't fooling Mom.

Her gaze fell to the box. "What's that?"

With reluctance, I handed it to her. "It's part of what I needed to talk to you about. It was left for me at the front desk this morning."

She lifted up the top, and her eyes widened. I could see her shocked gaze taking in the details. The white rose, green cellophane, red ribbon.

"Look at the card."

Mom pulled the card out of its envelope. For some time she stared at the words. Emotions played across her face — sadness ... regret ... confusion.

Firmly she replaced the card and lid, then plunked the box on the floor.

Mom laid her elbows on the arms of the chair. "It's not from him, if that's what you're thinking."

"How do you know?"

Her eyes roved across the room. "What I've told you is true, Shaley. He doesn't know about you. And besides, he couldn't send this."

A terrible thought gripped me. "Are you telling me he's *dead*?"

She shook her head.

"Then what?"

She pulled in a deep breath, then let it out. "I'm telling you it's not him."

Bitterness flooded me. "*Why* won't you just tell me the truth?" My voice turned off-key. "It's not *fair*. I have a right to know!"

Mom closed her eyes, and in that action, I saw myself. We were alike in so many ways, wanting to shut ourselves off from the world when we didn't like what we saw. Her fingers sank into the chair. "Let's talk about this later, okay?"

"You *always* say that."

"Shaley. Her tone hardened. "We have enough going on right now without bringing this up."

"*I* didn't bring it up. Whoever sent *that* did." I flung my arm toward the box. "And if it's not my dad, who is it? How would anyone else know?"

"You're not — "

A knock sounded at the door.

Mom turned her head toward it and sighed. "That'll be the detective."

I saw right through her — she was glad for the interruption. I pushed forward in my chair. "I'm not *what*, Mom? *Tell* me before you let him in."

She was already walking toward the door. Toward her excuse for not having to say anything more on the subject.

I shoved to my feet. "Mom!"

The sharp edge in my voice brought her to a halt. She turned three feet from the door, folded her arms, and gave me a long, pained look. In that moment, standing in her fancy hotel room, wearing my new designer jeans, I wished it would all go away. The tour, Rayne, the fame, the money, *everything*. I just wanted my mom, the way it used to be. And my dad. The three of us living together. Happy.

And I wanted Tom alive. Even if, without Rayne, I'd never have met him.

Mom studied the floor, then raised her chin. "Shaley, you're not the only one who knows about the rose."

Turning her back on me, she checked through the peephole, then opened the door to Detective Furlow.

21

The detective entered, and the atmosphere in the room shifted. Thoughts of my father morphed into memories of the previous night. Of Tom's still body, his missing eye. I slumped back into the armchair, wanting to hide. I wished I could be home in Southern California, in my own bedroom. We'd been on the road for three months, another one to go. It felt like an eternity.

Detective Furlow lumbered over behind Mom, carrying his notebook and a battered zipped binder. The tape recorder mocked me from his shirt pocket. Was the killer's voice, sounding innocent, captured in there during one of the detective's many interviews?

The idea sickened me.

Detective Furlow was dressed in the same clothes as last night, his shirt looking more rumpled than before. "Hi, Shaley."

I tried to dredge up a smile but couldn't. "Hi."

"Sorry I have to interrupt your afternoon like this."

"It's okay."

He stopped in the middle of the lounge area, glancing around as if not sure where to sit. Dark circles hung below his eyes. My heart panged at that.

"Haven't you slept?" From this angle he looked bigger than ever, like some heavyweight boxer. Or maybe he'd been a bodyguard back in the day.

One side of his large mouth curved. "Clothes give me away?"

"Kind of." I didn't want to say how bad he looked.

"Please." Mom gestured toward the loveseat facing our two arm-chairs. "Sit down."

"Thank you." He settled himself in the middle of the small couch, the two cushions spreading apart beneath his weight. He placed his binder and notebook on the table.

I swiveled my chair to face him more directly.

"No, I haven't slept," he said to me. "Haven't even been to bed." He shrugged. "It happens in a murder case. The first seventy-two hours are the most critical. If we don't apprehend the suspect in that time, the likelihood that we *will* find him decreases with every hour. So we keep at it."

Guilt washed through me as I watched him turn on the re-corder. While I'd slept and gone shopping to get my mind off Tom, this man had never stopped working to find his murderer. "What have you been doing all night?"

"Questioning people. Gathering evidence at the scene with the lab techs."

My fingers rubbed the arm of my chair. I'd swiveled enough that I couldn't see my purse on the floor, but the photo inside it practically screamed at me. Could it possibly be new evidence? Somehow connected to Tom's murder?

"Okay." Detective Furlow laced his fingers. "I'd like to get started now." He looked to Mom.

She nodded. "We really appreciate you coming here instead of us making us go to the station."

He raised his bushy eyebrows. "No problem. Easier that way, given the media following this case."

I thought of the reporters and paparazzi and shivered.

Detective Furlow switched on the recorder. He cited the date, time, and names of all present. He leaned forward, hands clasped, elbows on his knees. His notebook remained unopened. An almost apologetic expression creased his face.

He cleared his throat. "Shaley, I'm going to have to ask some questions that may not be comfortable for you. But I need your full cooperation."

Chills zigzagged between my shoulder blades. Mom's startled eyes flicked to me.

"One of the things I did early this morning was make a phone call to the jurisdiction where Tom lived." The detective examined his thumbs, one rubbing over the other as he spoke. "We asked officers first to notify Tom's next of kin. His mother lives in the area."

I dug my fingers into the chair, pulled momentarily from my own apprehension. Tom's poor mother. He'd talked to me about her more than once.

"Second, I wanted the officers to look around Tom's place. See what evidence they could find of relationships he was involved in. Often that information can lead to a suspect."

His thumb rubbed back and forth, back and forth. My skin started to tingle.

"Mrs. Hutchens didn't have a key to his place, so they had to break in. Since he lived alone, the officers were able to do that without a warrant. They got in early this afternoon."

All around us the air thickened. I sat very still.

The detective's thumbs stopped moving. He turned his head and looked deep into my eyes.

"Shaley, I know you're only sixteen, and Tom was twenty-five. That may have been your reason to keep the information from your mother. But I need to know now.

"Was Tom Hutchens your boyfriend?"

22

I stared at Detective Furlow, heat in my cheeks. My mom's heavily made-up eyes drilled into me like lasers. Her glossy red lips were pressed. The question was so unexpected, yet my tongue wouldn't move to deny it. It was a terrible feeling, their focus on me. As if *I'd* done something to cause Tom's murder.

"Shaley, what's going on?"

Mom's voice was steady but tight. She was pretty lenient about my dating. Had never kept me from having boyfriends. But I'd always gone out with guys from high school, and she knew about every one of them. She wouldn't have approved of someone Tom's age. The grim accusation on her face showed her disappointment that I'd kept this news from her. Even more, kept it from the detective last night.

I swallowed hard. Tearing my eyes away from Mom, I forced myself to look at the detective. "No. He wasn't my boyfriend. Ever. We didn't ... do anything like that. I mean *anything*. We were just good friends."

"Is that the truth, Shaley?" Mom demanded.

My throat half closed up, and my eyes burned. "*Yes*. I don't lie to you." My focus stayed on the detective. Would he even believe me?

Why had he asked in the first place?

Detective Furlow nodded, then gazed at the floor, as if dissecting my answer.

Air seeped from Mom's throat. She turned to him. "What did you find in Tom's apartment that made you ask?"

He unzipped his binder and withdrew an eight-by-ten glossy photo. "This."

Holding it horizontally, the detective handed it to Mom. She examined it closely, eyes roaming from side to side. Her forehead wrinkled.

"They were on the wall in Tom's bedroom," Detective Furlow said.

"What?" I thrust out my hand. Mom gave me the photo.

I leaned over it, feeling almost lightheaded. The photo showed a wall full of pictures. A whole montage of snapshots on Tom's wall. All of me. Or of us together. Some blown up, some regular size. Dozen and dozens of pictures.

Weaving around them in large letters, stretching across the entire length of the montage were the words, "I love Shaley."

The words stabbed me. I dropped my gaze to the floor.

Memories of Tom flashed through my head. His face close to mine as he leaned in to put liner on my eyes. His crooked smile at me across a room. The way he used to scarf down potato chips. His favorite flavor — barbecue. His laugh — deep from his chest. I always loved his laugh.

But, I didn't really *know* how he felt about me.

Had I caused him more pain than fun?

The photo burned in my hands. I leaned forward and pitched it onto the table.

"Shaley?" Mom scooted to the edge of her chair and leaned forward to touch my knee.

I shook my head and whispered, "I didn't know."

My arms folded. I looked down at my lap, my head spinning. It was too much to take in. I hated to admit it, but Tom had been right not to tell me. I never cared for him that way. If he'd said something, our friendship would never have been the same.

Mom sat back, her movements pulsing with protectiveness for me. I could have hugged her for that.

"All right, Detective." Her tone turned matter-of-fact. "This clearly isn't what you'd thought. So … does it now have any relevance to the case?"

Fleetingly, I wondered what difference it would have made even if I *had* been dating Tom.

Detective Furlow rubbed his jaw. "Don't know." He pulled in a long breath, let it out. "Tell me, does a white rose have any significance for either of you?"

23

Anger boiled inside him.

All afternoon TV reporters were talking about the murder. Flip the channel to a different news station, and there it was again.

It wasn't really the murder they cared about. What impact had Tom Hutchens's life had on greater society? What all the reporters and viewers alike wanted — all those *intrusive, gawking people* — was information on Rayne and Shaley O'Connor. How were they handling the murder? Were they close to the victim? Had they been spotted today?

When the reporters ran out of knowledgeable answers, they started speculating. Worse, they delved into Rayne's and Shaley's pasts. The fact that Rayne had remained single, had raised Shaley alone. The unknown factor of Shaley's father. *Yes*, they *dared* talk about such private things.

And *now* — see what they'd done. They accosted the Special One in public. Paparazzi hounded her, crowding around and scaring her to death.

Scum.

He wanted to kill every one of them.

That treatment of her was just as bad as Tom's lack of boundaries. Both sins threatened her. Neither could be tolerated.

Wincing, he rubbed between his eyes against a piercing headache, trying to calm himself. Now was not the time to let his guard down. Now ... was *not* ... the time.

But his hands itched, and his head throbbed.

This wasn't turning out as planned.

And the Special One herself—how deeply disappointing were her actions. What gratitude had she displayed for what he'd done? There she was, going on with her normal life. Going *shopping*! As if he hadn't sacrificed a thing for her. As if he hadn't put his own life on the line.

No, indeed. This wasn't turning out well.

It made him want to strangle somebody.

At Detective Furlow's question, I froze.

Mom stiffened. "Yes, a white rose has significance." She locked eyes with the detective, eyebrows raised, obviously waiting for an explanation before she gave hers. The white rose held too much symbolism and pain for her. She wasn't about to spill her story to just anyone — including the detective.

My eyes traveled to the box on the floor by Mom's chair.

Detective Furlow withdrew another photo from his binder and gave it to my mom. "This is the opposite wall in Tom's room."

Mom scooted forward in her chair and held it out so we could look together. I leaned toward her, afraid to look.

Dried white roses hung on Tom's wall, surrounding another, smaller mural made from pictures of me. Three roses in all. Each wrapped in green cellophane and tied with a red ribbon.

I shoved the photo away, violation spinning through my gut. This was going *way* too far. The very symbol that represented my father's love for Mom. How *dare* Tom use it! How dare he put white roses on the wall of his apartment — for *me*! He couldn't possibly have felt for me what my father felt for my mom. No way. The union of the white rose had *created* me.

Mom placed the photo on the table, her jaw tight.

The detective looked from me to Mom. "What does it mean?"

Mom looked at the floor. "The first time I saw a white rose wrapped that way, it was on my doorstep with a note. It was from Shaley's father. We were in high school. I was fifteen; he was seventeen. As we dated, I'd find similar white roses, always with the same note about how special I was to him ..."

Her words drifted away.

I drew in my shoulders. It felt so wrong hearing my mom tell the detective this. It was too private, the cause of too many arguments between her and me.

Abruptly, Mom picked the boxed rose off the floor and set it on the table before the detective. Took off the lid. "This was delivered to Shaley this morning."

The detective surveyed the rose, no hint of surprise on his face.

I reached into my purse and pulled out the "always watching" photo. "I have something too. I didn't get a chance to show you this yet, Mom. I just found it this afternoon." I laid it beside the boxed rose. "The message on the back is kind of the same."

"What is it?" Mom pushed forward in her chair, ready to snatch it up.

"Wait." The detective held his hand protectively over the picture. "Don't touch it."

He stood up and fished in his front pants pocket. Pulled out a pair of latex gloves and put them on. I sat woodenly, feeling like I'd fallen into some TV crime drama. Bruce, Brittany, and I would have fingerprints all over that photo, maybe obliterating the ones that counted. Mom leaned toward the table, trying to decipher the photo upside down.

Detective Furlow sat again. Straightening the picture with one gloved finger, he bent low and frowned at it. He glanced up at me, then turned it around for Mom to see.

Her jaw slackened.

"Where was this taken?" He looked from her to me.

Mom stared at the photo. "Last night, right here in the parking lot as we arrived. But I didn't see *anyone*. Did you, Shaley?"

I shook my head.

The detective narrowed his eyes. "Looks dark, like it was taken without a flash." With his index finger, he flipped it over.

"Always watching." Mom read the words aloud. She snapped her head toward me, cheeks flushed. "Where'd you get this?"

"When all the paparazzi and reporters crowded me at the mall, somebody put it in my bag."

Detective Furlow focused on the boxed rose. With his gloved hands, he examined the envelope and card. Finished, he replaced everything as he'd found it.

He opened his notebook and slid a pen from his binder.

"You said you recognized some of the photographers at the mall, Shaley?"

"Yes, some of them, but I don't know all their real names." I related Mom's and my nicknames for them, and the tabloids they worked for.

Mom's expression hardened. "I can't stand those people. Any one of them could have put that picture in Shaley's bag. They're that low."

"Why do you think they would do that?" the detective asked.

"Because all they care about is getting 'the picture.' Something no one else has. Or finding some personal information about us that no one else knows. It's all about the money. They find that stuff, and they get paid a lot for it." She shook her head. "I'm telling you, they don't even think of us — or anyone else famous — as people. We're just photo ops for them. Especially Vulture."

"What happened with him?"

Mom told the detective about the stakeouts at our house, and the lies Vulture's tabloid had told.

When she finished, the three of us fell silent. Detective Furlow sat on the edge of the cushions, one huge hand cupping his jaw. His gaze traveled from the rose ... to the photo of Tom's wall ... to the "always watching" picture of me. Then around the circle again.

Mom and I exchanged uneasy glances.

The detective scratched his cheek and frowned.

"What are you thinking?" Mom demanded.

The detective looked up, his gaze traveling past Mom, over her shoulder, as if he read writing on the wall. "We'll try to trace who sent the flower. The florist's name is on the card. Someone had to order the rose and pay for it. Let's hope it was paid for with a credit card, not by cash in person."

"I already called the florist. It *was* paid for by credit card, but the stupid lady wouldn't tell me the buyer's name."

Detective Furlow's eyebrows rose. "You thought to do that? Good work."

I made a face. "Didn't lead to anything. No matter how I begged, she wouldn't tell me." I managed a vengeful smile. "Guess it'll be a little different when a detective asks."

Righteous indignation creased Mom's forehead. She stared at the detective. "You're thinking the same person sent both of those, aren't you?" She pointed to the rose and photo. "One of those *detestable* paparazzi is stalking my daughter."

He hesitated. "I would guess that the rose and photo are connected. But those two things so close to Tom Hutchens's murder …" He gestured to the picture of Tom's wall with the white roses. "I'm wondering if the same person is behind *all three*."

I'd wondered the same thing. But how? Why?

Mom shook her head. "There were no paparazzi backstage last night. They never could have gotten through security."

"True," he said.

"And it's unlikely that any local union worker who would have been backstage could have followed us to the hotel to take Shaley's picture. Even though we left late, all the hired workers had been delayed by everything that happened. They still would have been packing up our equipment."

"Yes."

Mom focused across the room. When she spoke again, her voice was grim. "Which means you're thinking it's someone who's part of our tour."

S omeone on the tour? The mere idea was horrifying.
  "I don't believe it," I declared.

Detective Furlow inclined his head. "I know that's hard to think about. But for the sake of your safety" — he gestured from Mom to me — "you need to know that's where my suspicions lie."

"You mean someone *here* — with us at the hotel?" Mom pressed. "Because all the people on the bus are long gone on their way to Denver."

"Not necessarily someone here. Also we can't assume only one person is involved. One person could have killed Tom — and maybe ordered that white rose ahead of time to be sent to Shaley. But someone else could have put the photo in her shopping bag this afternoon."

Mom frowned. "But then Shaley would have recognized the person." She turned to me. "Did you see anyone from the tour at the mall?"

"No. Well, only Bruce, of course."

"Your bodyguard?" the detective asked.

"Yes."

He mulled over the information. "Is it possible you could have missed someone in the crowd? Maybe someone who could have sneaked up behind you, dropped that picture in the bag, and faded away?"

I bit my cheek, remembering the crush of people. All the flashes and questions and yelling. "I guess that could have happened. But again, Bruce was there. He didn't see anyone from the tour either."

At least not that he told me about.

The thought punched me in the gut. *Bruce.* He'd waited outside the dressing room all that time. Had *he* made phone calls that brought the paparazzi? Had he staged a crowd around me so he could slip something into my bag unnoticed?

No. I couldn't believe that. Not Bruce. Not someone that close to me and Mom.

Detective Furlow watched the emotions play across my face as if reading my every thought.

I raised my chin. "It couldn't be Bruce, if that's what you're thinking." My voice wavered, and that ticked me off. My brain sped through the timeline of Tom's murder, seeking proof.

No, wait.

"Bruce was right there when we got out of the limo last night," I said. "So there's no way he could have taken that picture of me."

"That's true — he was with us." Mom spoke the words slowly, with an edge. The idea that Tom's murderer could be someone she knew, someone she worked with every day, clearly petrified her.

The detective spread his hands. "These are just theories. I don't want to rule out anything. Maybe these three things are connected, maybe they aren't. Maybe two people are working together, which obviously means one person wouldn't have to be in all the places. Again, I'm only telling you this to say, *be careful.* Don't assume when you fly on to your next concert tomorrow that you're leaving the perpetrator behind in San Jose."

His words hung in the air.

You're wrong, I told him in my head. *You are wrong.* "You're not going to say this to any reporters, are you — that you think it's someone on tour?" One opinion like that on the news, and Brittany's mom would have her on the next plane home.

"No, no. I don't divulge details of an ongoing investigation."

Still, what if TV news people started saying that? They were already throwing out all kinds of opinions about the crime.

Mom shifted in her chair. "But why the photo of Shaley, anyway? What would that have to do with Tom's murder?"

Detective Furlow drummed his huge fingers on the coffee table, as if deciding how much to say.

He focused on Mom. "If we look at the murder and these 'watching' messages together, they could hint at a motive."

Cold prickles crept across the back of my neck. "What kind of motive?"

The detective lifted a hand. "Now that we know how Tom felt about you, if someone else found that out, maybe a jealous someone …"

My jaw hinged open, and my whole body numbed. Was he saying it was *my* fault Tom was dead? Someone killed him … because of *me*?

No way. I couldn't live with that knowledge. *Ever.*

I shoved to my feet. "You're *wrong!*" I hurled the words at Detective Furlow, my body stiff and shoulders cocked back. "You're wrong, and I'll never believe it!"

Nausea rolled up my throat. I pressed a hand to my mouth.

"Shaley—" Mom reached for me.

I shook my head hard, stepped out of her reach. My stomach rolled.

Swiveling on one foot, I stumbled toward the connecting door to my room. I hit it hard and bounced off. Then I grabbed the knob and twisted. Leaping into my room, I slammed the door behind me.

"Shaley!" Brittany jumped off her bed. "What *happened*?"

I couldn't stop. Couldn't even look at her. My feet moved under me, weaving, headed for the bathroom. Falling on my knees before the toilet, I slammed up its seat … and threw up.

Out of the bathroom, flat on my back on the bed, I felt weak and depleted. My tears wouldn't stop. Once I started crying, I cried for everything wrong in my life — past and present. Missing Tom, the nightmare of seeing his dead face, the horrible afternoon, my sadness that Mom didn't have the time for me she used to have, and my years-long wish to know my dad. Even with Brittany to console me, the emptiness was too much all at once.

When a break in my tears finally came, I longed to talk to Mom like we used to do when I was younger. But she was probably still with Detective Furlow. Besides, the gap between us had grown. I didn't know *how* to go to her with my biggest heartaches anymore.

Carly. That's who I could call.

I looked up the number to the room she shared with Lois and Melissa and phoned, hoping she hadn't gone out to dinner. My heart flip-flopped when Carly answered.

"Hi," I choked, "it's Shaley. Can you come to my room for a minute?" I didn't want to go to hers in case her roommates were there.

"Sure, baby. I'll be right over."

When a knock sounded on the door, Brittany checked through the peephole before opening up. From my slumped position on my bed, I watched Carly hustle inside, all open arms and compassion. She was dressed in jeans and an old red T-shirt with gold letters on the front spelling TRUTH. No makeup. She headed straight for me, sat down, put her arm around my shoulders, and pulled me close.

I leaned against her, fresh tears biting my eyes. She smelled faintly of the jasmine-scented body lotion she always wore. Brittany sat on her own bed, facing us.

Even then, Carly asked no questions. She simply let me cry, her right hand rubbing my upper arm. "Jesus, Jesus," she whispered, "please comfort this dear child."

I wasn't sure how Jesus could comfort me. He was in heaven; I was stuck here on earth. And at that moment it was a lousy place to be.

My hand rose to flick away tears. Brittany fetched me a tissue. As I took it from her, a thought pierced me. Maybe Jesus used other people to comfort. Carly and Brittany were doing a good job of it.

I cried myself out, then straightened, shuddering a breath. My head hurt. The wet tissue balled in my fingers. Carly scooted away a little and shifted to face me. Her dark eyes glistened. "Ready to tell me about it?"

It spilled from me in a torrent, Brittany filling in details. The white rose. Paparazzi and reporters in the mall. The photo in my shopping bag. Tom's apartment wall, full of pictures. Detective Furlow's thought that Tom could have been killed because of *me*.

"Because of you?" Carly's head drew back. "Surely he didn't put it like that."

"Might as well have. He said maybe someone found out how Tom felt about me and was jealous."

"Shaley." Carly put her finger under my chin, nudging me to look her in the eye. "If someone killed Tom for that reason — and we don't even know if that's the case — that person is crazy. He's misguided and evil. You *cannot* take responsibility for such a person's actions. It wasn't *your* fault. And it wasn't Tom's fault for caring about you." She smiled. "There's got to be hundreds of guys out there who feel the same way about you, just by looking at your picture."

I sniffed. "But it was more than that. Tom … *loved* me. At least that's what he put on his wall. How could I not know?"

"Because he didn't want you to. Maybe he would have told you someday. Maybe not."

I sighed and lowered my eyes. Rubbed my finger across patterned stitching in the bedspread. Brittany pulled her feet up and sat cross-legged.

My stomach rumbled. Lunch had been over seven hours ago, and after my flight to the bathroom, there was nothing left in me. Still, I couldn't imagine eating.

"All of this, Carly. It makes me feel so ... unsure of things. Like I can't really control anything in my life. And I can't even be sure of what I know. I didn't understand how Tom felt. I don't know anything more about my dad. I don't know what's going to happen tomorrow."

Carly inhaled a long breath. "None of us do, Shaley. That's why we need God so much."

A new expression flickered over her face, mixing anger and righteous defiance. Her tone firmed. "And listen to me, Shaley. Someone meant those words on the back of that photo to harm you. But here's the good news. Someone *is* always watching. That someone is Jesus. He's watching when things are good and when things are terrible. I should know; I've been through both. So every time those words ring in your head, Shaley, don't just think of the mean person in this world who wrote them. Think of God in heaven, because that's his promise to you."

I brushed at imagined lint on my jeans, fighting the urge to steal a look at Brittany. I hadn't asked Carly here to talk about God. But I should have known she would.

"Can I tell you something about my own life?" Carly asked after a moment.

I nodded.

She remained silent. I looked at her and saw memories — whatever they might be — creasing her face. She focused on the distance, beyond the room, as if the walls had disappeared and she gazed into her past.

"I lost my mama when I was nine."

I blinked in surprise. Brittany made a sad sound in her throat.

"My father was an alcoholic. He went over the deep end after Mama died. He lost his job. Couldn't provide for me. I didn't have brothers or sisters, so I felt very alone when he stayed out all night drinking. He ended up robbing a bank. They caught him, and he went to jail. I was, for all practical purposes, an orphan."

Oh. I squeezed her arm. Losing *both* parents was more than I could imagine. "What did you do?"

"My grandmama took me in." Carly smiled. "She was a praying woman. She prayed over me loud and long. Downright shook the rafters. I thought she was a little crazy, but I loved her. She was so good to me." Carly looked at her lap. "I only had her a year. Then she died too."

I shook my head. So much loss. I never would have guessed this about Carly.

"After that I was shoved in and out of foster homes, all the way until I graduated from high school." Carly's voice dropped. "Those years were terrible. I can't tell you how bad. I *won't* tell you all that happened to me. I thought I'd lost everything. I *had* lost everything — on this earth. But in my senior year of high school, I found the most important thing. I realized that Jesus loves me, and I will always have him, no matter what I have to face. After that I turned to him for guidance every day."

Have him? Didn't seem much good to me since you can't even see Jesus. How do you turn to someone for guidance when you can't see him?

"If Jesus loves you, why'd he let all those things happen?"

Carly sighed. "Baby, I don't know. I figure I'll understand when I get to heaven. But I do think it's the wrong question to focus on. We *know* this world can be hard to get through. The right question is, what are you going to do about that? If you were on a long, hard trip, wouldn't you want a map to guide you? If you wanted to put a model car together, wouldn't you read the instructions? God *created* this world, including us. Jesus is our map, our instruction booklet. If we go it alone, we're bound to have a much harder time."

I trailed a painted fingernail across the bedspread. "Did things get better for you after you turned to God?"

"No. Not for a while. I fell in love with a man who cheated on me. He broke my heart. Then I lost a couple of jobs and practically had to live on the street." She shook her head. "Life was tough. But with God's help I *did* get better at handling things. I began to see he had a purpose in allowing me to go through hard times. Those times brought me closer to him, because I had to rely on him more."

It sounded good. I wanted what Carly had. I wanted to *believe* in something bigger than myself. Bigger than my circumstances. Especially after the circumstances of that day. But something in my heart balled up like the wet tissue in my hand.

What little energy I possessed evaporated from my limbs. I shivered and crossed my arms.

Carly surveyed me. "You're tired, poor thing. Have you eaten?"

My lips twisted into a sick expression. I glanced at Brittany. "No."

"Well, honey, you need to do that. Order some room service. Put some meat on those bones, as my grandmother would say."

Her mouth curved. I gave her a tiny smile back.

"Thanks, Carly." I hugged her. "You're the best."

She pushed off the bed. "Call me if you need me now, hear? Any time." She looked from me to Brittany. "I'll see you tomorrow on the way to the airport, if not before."

We had a ten a.m. call to meet the limos. Our flight to Denver was at 11:55.

"Okay. Thanks again, Carly."

She slipped out the door.

Brittany gave me a tired smile. "Carly's nice."

"Yeah. The best."

We looked at each other, saying no more. But I knew she was wondering about the Jesus thing, as I was.

I checked the digital clock on the night stand. Its red numbers said 7:45. I was so tired. This day felt like a thousand hours already.

Brittany rubbed her flat stomach. "I'm starved. Can you eat something?"

"I'll try." As I walked over to the desk for the large black binder that contained the room service menu, my mom's voice flashed through my brain.

You're not the only one who knows about the rose.

I fingered the pages of the binder. Who else knew? And how?

The shrimp and pasta Brittany and I ordered was delivered by a young waiter with thick black hair and ice-blue eyes. He looked like he belonged more on the movie screen than pushing room-service carts. He set the covered plates and drinks on a table by the window.

"There you are, Miss O'Connor." He dipped his head to me, then Brittany.

"Thank you." I nudged a five-dollar bill into his hand.

"Appreciate it." He raised his cool eyes and gazed at me.

The moment stretched out, and still he looked. Electricity danced up my nerves. I pulled back, tensing. "What?"

He gestured toward my hair. "I like you better without the wig."

Abruptly he swiveled toward the empty cart and pushed it toward the door, as if realizing he'd overstepped his bounds. I stared after him as he slipped out into the hall.

The door clicked shut.

I turned to Brittany, feeling violated all over again. "We already made the news."

"Yeah. Terrific."

I focused on the black screen of the TV. The last thing I wanted was to see the coverage and be reminded of those awful minutes in the mall. But to not know what reporters were saying ...

Striding to the nightstand, I snatched up the TV remote and punched the *on* button.

From the table, the smell of pasta and cream sauce wafted up my nose. My stomach flip-flopped.

"Go ahead and eat." My face scrunched up. Gripping the remote, I flipped channels to find the news stations.

"That's okay, I'll wait for you."

"No, Brittany. *Eat.*"

I pushed the channel button.

A car commercial.

Brittany sat down at the table and angled toward the TV.

Punch.

A sitcom.

Punch.

MTV.

Punch.

News. Something about the economy.

Come on!

My index finger worked feverishly, my stiff arm thrust toward the TV. With every channel, the dread inside me grew. I'd shouted at the reporters and burst into tears. They'd probably shown it over and over — made me look as bad and weak as possible. What great drama for all the watchers across America.

Had I hurt the band? Would Mom be mad at me?

Brittany took a few bites, then clacked down her fork. The sound shot right through me.

"Wait," she said. "Maybe it's not on at all."

"Then how would he know?"

"Maybe he was *there.*"

My hand dropped, the remote dangling from my fingers. A cell phone ad played on the TV. "But I don't remember seeing him. Do you?"

"No. Not that it means much. There were so many people ..."

We locked eyes, trying to think it through. If the waiter had been there — what could it mean?

"Wouldn't he have been here, working?" Brittany asked.

"I don't know. Maybe he works dinner to closing."

My gaze traveled to the connecting door to Mom's room. Mentally I rehashed the conversation with Detective Furlow. Pictured him turning over the "always watching" photo with his gloved hand.

I blew out a breath. "I'm going to keep checking."

Brittany ate. I sank onto my bed and channel surfed between the news stations.

Suddenly, there we were on the screen. I gasped.

"Leave me alone!" I watched myself cry. The cameras flashed, the crowd pressed in. Microphones were thrust at me. And the expression on my face! I looked so scared, like some homeless child with nowhere to run. Just watching the scene, I felt the claustrophobia crowding my lungs.

I shuddered.

The camera panned over Bruce as he pushed through the crowd, then focused on Brittany. Her features were pinched and white.

"Oh, no." She pushed her plate away. "My mom's going to freak."

My throat tightened. "Will she make you go home?"

"Probably."

"But you said you *can't*."

"I know. I won't."

"What is it, Brittany? What's going to happen to me if you leave?"

"I told you I don't know for sure. Just ... something. Some danger."

I huffed. "What good is sensing the future if you can't be a little more specific?"

"Maybe," she said grimly, "we don't want to know."

I cast her a long look, then turned back to the TV. A camera captured the three of us bursting out the door and jumping into the black limo. The last scene showed the car driving away.

"Did you see the waiter anywhere in that crowd?" I asked.

"No. But the footage was pretty fast. He still could have been there."

A blonde female commentator filled the screen, relating the known details of Tom's death and the investigation. A detective was interviewed — not Detective Furlow. He didn't say much except that they were "following a few leads."

The report ended.

"We could call the hotel restaurant," Brittany said. "Ask somebody if that waiter was working this afternoon."

I tilted my head. "But he'd probably hear that we asked. I don't want him to know we're suspicious of him."

"What are we suspicious *of* anyway? Even if he was in the mall, he couldn't have been backstage last night. He couldn't have had anything to do with Tom's death."

"Remember, the detective said more than one person could be involved." I wandered to the bed, sank down on it, and stared at the ceiling. All these puzzle pieces. I felt way too frazzled. My tired mind couldn't begin to sort it all out. "I don't know. I just *don't know.*"

With a deep sigh, I turned onto my side in a fetal position. Another whiff of shrimp filled my nostrils. No way could I eat it now, even though my body needed food. I just wanted to go to sleep and wake up when this was all over. Like maybe a year from now.

A knock sounded on the connecting door.

Mom.

"It's open!" I dragged myself off the bed to face her.

Mom stepped inside. Her eyes flicked over Brittany and the food, then roved across my face. "Shaley, are you okay?"

Can't you see I'm not?

I shrugged. "Yeah."

Her gaze held mine. *Ask me again, Mom. Ask me again.*

She checked her watch. "I've set a meeting for all of us here in the hotel. It's in ten minutes in Ross's room."

"Why?"

"There are things we need to talk about."

"You mean Tom's death?"

"Partly."

I drew back. "You going to tell them about his wall? That it's my fault he's dead?"

Mom's face softened. She touched my arm. "Shaley, this is *not* your fault."

"But I don't want them to know!"

I couldn't imagine it — Ross and the bodyguards and everyone in the band looking at me. Hearing what Tom had felt. Just thinking about it, I wanted to throw up all over again.

"I'm not going to tell them that. In fact the detective wants it kept quiet. But we do need to talk about added media attention. That, on top of the murder — we all need to be extra careful."

I shrank away. "Are you going to tell everybody about the white rose? And the 'always watching' photo? I don't want them to know that either."

"Shaley, you just might be in danger, don't you understand? For some reason *you've* been targeted with these things. I want the rest of the band to know that much. We can all help watch out for you."

"We've got Mick and Wendell and Bruce for that. Besides, what can happen to me behind a locked hotel door?"

Mom's eyes closed. "It's not just tonight. It's tomorrow and the day after that." She held on to both my shoulders. "I'm *not* going to let anything happen to you."

"Why not?" The words blurted out of me, bitter and cold. "Then you wouldn't have to keep all the stuff about my dad from me anymore."

Mom pulled in a sharp breath. Her eyes glistened. "That has nothing to do with this. I just want to keep you safe."

Deep down I knew that was true. But trust can't be put into separate boxes. If I couldn't trust Mom for one piece of my life — the piece that involved my father and who he was and who that made *me* — I couldn't trust her in others.

"Shaley, *talk* to me. You know I love you."

The back of my throat burned. I didn't want to cry. "I love you too."

She squeezed my shoulders, then let go, all business once more. She had band issues to attend to. "We can finish this conversation later. Right now we need to get over to Ross's room."

I turned my head away, my gaze landing on the food. Brittany had eaten most of hers. Mine hadn't been touched.

My chest deflated. "Brittany's coming with me, Mom."

No way was I going through this torture without her.

Ross's room was a suite even bigger than Mom's, complete with a work area containing a large desk, fax, and multiple phone lines. We all crowded into that space, pulling chairs away from a rectangular table, pushing the couches and love seat into a haphazard circle. Brittany and I sat on two chairs as far back as possible.

I swear I could have cut the tension in that room with a knife.

Maybe most of it was mine.

Ross perched on the black desk chair, his short, heavy legs spread apart and belly hanging over his jeans. One strand of his scraggly brown hair hung in his face. He'd shot me a long look as Brittany and I entered. "Shaley, how you doing?"

Just great. I tossed him a tiny smile.

Kim and Morrey, Rayne's drummer, sat together, holding hands. Morrey wore a plain white T-shirt, revealing his tattooed arms. His full lips were pressed together, dark hair in a ponytail. His face looked strained.

Rich, the bass player, was next to Mom on one couch. He leaned back with hands clasped behind his shaved head and knobby elbows sticking out. His casual pose turned my stomach. How could he look so relaxed in a meeting about Tom's murder?

Stan, the lead guitarist, was pitched forward on the other couch, feet wide apart and black hands dangling between his knees. He frowned at the carpet, glancing up now and then as others walked in.

Bruce, Wendell, and Mick stood, leaving the seats for everyone else. Carly came with Melissa and Lois. She smiled at me and mouthed, "You okay?"

I hesitated, then nodded.

"Okay, let's start." Mom ran a hand through her hair. "First, all cell phones off. Not vibrate. *Off.* I don't want this meeting interrupted."

Everyone took out their phones and powered them down. Musical tones collided with each other, then the room fell silent.

Mom looked from one face to another, her gaze snagging on me. My eyes pleaded even then for her to say nothing. To just say we all needed to be careful, as Detective Furlow still didn't have a firm suspect. That's all she needed to reveal.

Please, Mom.

She held my eyes a moment longer. I could practically hear the wheels of decision turning in her head. Stan straightened, looking from her to me, questions in his expression.

Mom laid a hand at the back of her neck. "Some things happened today — involving Shaley."

I slumped down in my seat. Briefly Mom told them about the delivered flower and photo with similar messages. She left out the detail of the white rose.

Rich twisted around to look at me in surprise. "Shaley, this is terrible. I'm so sorry."

I lowered my eyes.

"I don't know what all this means," Mom said. "Maybe they're just coincidences with Tom's death. But the timing ..."

Ross slapped his hands on his meaty thighs. "Whatever's going on, we're going to be watching Shaley extra carefully. Wendell, Bruce, Mick — she doesn't go anywhere without being guarded. And that means so much as step out her hotel room door."

Mick and Wendell nodded, faces unsmiling. Bruce said, "Yes, sir."

I gripped my upper arms. *Please, Mom, keep your word and don't say anything about Tom's wall.*

Mom gave me a purposeful look. Her mouth tightened, blue eyes narrowing. And she blinked slowly. It was a look to say, *I know what you're thinking. And I'm not going to tell them.*

My throat cinched up, tears of relief biting my eyes.

The meeting went on for another hour, people venting opinions over who killed Tom. Morrey insisted it had to be a local roadie. "Somebody got through that back door, that's all there is to it." He rubbed the Superman tattoo on his upper left arm. "If I were the detective, I'd be questioning the local guard posted at that door real hard. Maybe he *let* someone through."

"Or what about any fan who wanted to get backstage?" Rich spread his hands. "Maybe one of the inside security people let the guy through."

"Who says it's a guy?" Ross raised his eyebrows. Carly looked at him askance. He shrugged. "I'm just saying — we don't know."

Rich wagged his head. "Guy, girl. Either way, that means a mere thirty thousand people attending the concert are suspects."

"Maybe Tom was into something we don't know about," Stan said. "Like drugs. Someone could have killed him over that."

No way, Tom hated drugs. I shot Stan a disgusted look.

"Or maybe he knew something he shouldn't know." Morrey scuffed a sneakered foot against the carpet. "I've seen that happen before. Remember Stephen Restler who played with Ace? He was going to testify against some gang member and was shot before the trial started."

Kim stuck a hand in her hair. "Did Tom gamble? Owe somebody too much money?"

No, he didn't gamble.

I pressed my legs together, teeth clenched. What was *wrong* with everybody? Didn't they know Tom better than that?

Shaley — you didn't know him either.

The thought hit me like a brick. I pushed back against the chair, feeling sick all over again. True, I didn't know him like I'd thought.

What other secrets had Tom kept from me? Maybe he *did* do drugs. Gamble. Hang out with violent people.

My eyes flicked from one face to another — to the people I thought I knew so well. What were *they* hiding from me? From the rest of us?

What if one of them *was* the murderer?

Revulsion shot up my spine. No, I couldn't believe that.

Kim blew out air. "You know, Tom might have — "

"Stop it!" I shoved up from the chair. "Stop it, all of you! You don't know what you're saying. There wasn't anything wrong with Tom — there *wasn't*."

My chin quivered. *No.* I did *not* want anyone to see me cry.

"Shaley." Mom stood up. "We didn't mean — "

"I don't want to hear it. I just — I'm *leaving*." Shuddering a breath, I stalked across the room. Behind me, I heard the rustle of Brittany pushing to her feet.

Mick strode to the door, opened it, and checked in the hallway. "Okay." He motioned me out, his expression a total poker face.

I flounced from the room, not looking back. Brittany followed.

Mick escorted us down the hall, took my key card and slid it into the lock. Inside our room, he checked around the beds and in the bathroom before pronouncing it safe.

When he left, I collapsed on my bed, feeling numb.

Thank goodness Brittany was with me. I wouldn't want to face this night alone.

By sheer habit, Brittany pulled out her cell phone and turned it on.

She groaned. "Oh, no. I have a message from Mom."

He collapsed on his bed and shut his eyes, blocking out external sound. This day had been long and hard—and it wasn't over yet. He needed sleep, but he wouldn't get it. His back was tied in knots, and his neck felt like stone. Tension squeezed at his veins and arteries. His head still pounded.

Every Saturday he received a call from the person who had sent him on this tour to watch the Special One. In the past their conversations had been brief and veiled—there was a risk that others could be listening. He spoke of his work like he was just shooting the breeze, knowing the person on the other end of the line understood the meaning behind his chatter.

But now he no longer took the calls. Nor would he ever again. Things weren't going exactly the way the sender had planned.

The scene of the Special One at the mall flashed repeatedly through his brain.

Such chances for her he'd taken—and she'd gone *shopping*.

He pictured her tears as the crowd hemmed in, the fear on her face. Maybe she was a little too ungrateful. Maybe she'd deserved that.

And the lurid details he remembered of that crowd. Especially the close, pressed bodies ...

He cycled his legs against the mattress, seeking comfort that couldn't be found.

Face it—he never should have agreed to this mission. Sure, the sender's money was good, but the *ungratefulness* of this girl. The sheer *flaunting* of herself — in front of the whole world.

He'd thought she was as superior as he. That she deserved him. How wrong he was.

Brittany had to go home.

Her mother was adamant. She wasn't going to have her daughter hounded and scared by the press. She never should have let Brittany come in the first place.

I curled up on my bed, worn and hungry, and listened to Brittany's side of the conversation.

"I wasn't *that* scared, Mom. It was really no big deal."

"But they have bodyguards with us *all the time*."

"So *what*! We didn't think they'd notice Shaley in the wig. But now it doesn't matter, because her mom already told us we're not going anywhere. And we're *guarded*."

"I can't leave her now; she needs me. I *won't* go."

I don't know what'll happen, Shaley, just ... some danger.

"All the other people on tour don't matter. I'm her *best friend*. I need to stay with her."

"We're leaving San Jose tomorrow, remember? We'll be in Colorado, far away from whoever killed Tom."

Let's hope so.

"How am I supposed to get home anyway? Rayne's already paid for all my plane tickets. I've already got one for Denver."

Her mom had already figured that out. Brittany would ride in the limo with us to the airport in the morning. Instead of boarding the plane to Denver, she'd be catching one a half hour later bound for Southern California. End of story.

Brittany stomped back and forth across the room, begging and pleading and arguing until she was practically blue in the face. "Do I have to get Rayne to talk to you again? Is *that* what it's going to take?"

"Mom, I *can't* leave. I'm telling you, she *needs* me here."

I pulled a pillow over my head, wishing I could shut out her voice. Her arguments wouldn't matter, I knew that. Future lawyer or not, this time she wouldn't be changing her mother's mind.

In the end, Brittany smacked off the call, threw her phone across the room, and sank down on her bed. She lowered her head and started to cry silently. I sat up cross-legged, watching her shoulders shake. My tears had all dried up. I was just too tired.

Brittany sniffed. "I can't believe this."

"I can. After all that's happened? I wouldn't expect *anything* to go right."

Brittany spread her fingers on the bedspread and bunched up the fabric. "Maybe you could come home with me."

My stomach grumbled. I still hadn't eaten anything. When we came back to the room, my dinner was too cold. We'd set our plates outside in the hall.

"Do you think you could?" Brittany looked at me, her face pinched.

"I wish. I can't *wait* to go home. But I know what Mom would say. Here I'm close to her, plus we have the bodyguards. There I wouldn't have any protection."

"Maybe Bruce could come with you."

Wouldn't that be *great*? To go home and see all my friends again.

"But your mom wouldn't want me staying with you. I'd just bring trouble."

Brittany considered that. "You could stay at your own house. Your housekeeper's there. Bruce or Wendell could even stay in one of your guest bedrooms."

I fastened a look on her, feeling a twist in my belly. Brittany's eyes held mine. Slowly her expression flattened.

"You don't think …"

"No. But how can I know for sure? Detective Furlow thinks Tom's killer is one of us. How can I know it's not Bruce or Wendell or Mick?"

"But you *know* them. You *trust* them."

"I thought I knew Tom too. I didn't."

"But that's diff — "

"Brittany, *shut up*." My voice thinned to steel. I pushed off the bed, hands thrust in my hair. "You think I want to have these thoughts? That I want to distrust everyone around me? This is driving me *crazy*."

She dropped her head, pressed thumb and forefinger between her eyes. I took a few aimless steps, then flopped back down on the mattress.

"Sorry." I cast her a rueful look. "Didn't mean to snap at you."

"I know." She sighed. "At least ask your mom. Would you just do that?"

So I asked. I didn't even want to drag myself to the connecting door. Instead I turned on my phone and called Mom's cell. I told Mom Brittany had to leave and begged halfheartedly to go with her, knowing the answer.

"No. You need to stay near me. Near the bodyguards. *No way* am I letting you take off on your own."

Depression weighing me down, I hung up. Brittany and I barely spoke. We hugged each other, then went about the business of packing. I wished I hadn't bought any new clothes. Now I just had to work all the harder at fitting things in my suitcase.

We watched a movie. I hardly saw it.

Sometime after eleven we crawled into bed, craving sleep but dreading tomorrow.

We turned out the lights, and I stared upward, reliving the last twenty-four hours — finding Tom, the nightmare about my father. The rose, the photo, the crushing crowd.

Sweaty and trembling, I took a long time going to sleep.

Troubled dreams wove through my head, surreal scenes of the

mall and flashing cameras, white roses raining down on me, walls covered with pictures materializing out of nowhere —

And a blasting sound in my ears, loud enough to wake the dead. My eyes flew open.

The *blat-blat-blat* pitched raucous and high. Blaring again and again. The noise took an ice pick to my head. I jerked upright in bed, smacking both hands over my ears.

"What *is* it?" Brittany shouted.

I sucked in deep breaths. "A fire alarm!"

Blat-blat-blat. I squeezed my eyes shut.

"Shaley, what do we do?"

It wasn't the first time I'd heard a fire alarm in a hotel. I pulled back the covers and forced my feet to the floor. "We have to get out of here!" I stood up, swaying, my body groggy and heavy.

Blat-blat-blat. The noise was about to burst my brain open.

Brittany groaned. "Maybe it's a false alarm."

"We can't rely on that. Besides, you want to stay and listen to this?"

"No." Brittany slid out of bed.

We switched on a lamp, blinking in the sudden light, and slipped into the clothes we'd taken off just a few hours ago. My arms and legs were limbering up. I shoved my feet into my shoes, remembering to grab my room key from the nightstand. "Ready?"

Brittany flipped uncombed hair from her face. "Yeah!"

Mom pounded on the connecting door. I leapt for it and swung it open.

Mom stood in shorts and a T-shirt, tension in her every movement. "Come with me." She swiveled toward her room.

Brittany and I scurried after her.

Blat-blat-blat.

"You're not going out there alone!" Mom yelled over her shoulder as we hurried through her room. "Mick's outside, ready to take us down. Shaley, don't you *move* from his side."

We slammed through the door and into the hall, then ran for the stairwell, Mick beside me. The noise was every bit as loud out there as in our rooms.

As he ran, Mick's right hand hovered waist high, near the gun he always wore beneath his shirt.

Rooms slid by in peripheral vision. Other band members popped out of their doors, joining us in our flight.

Mick's right fingers flexed.

We reached the steps. With no food in my stomach, I felt so weak. My legs started to wobble on the very first flight. We had fourteen floors to go down.

Blat-blat-blat. The alarm ricocheted off the hard stairs and metal railing, the stark white walls. Echoes bounced around my aching head, their vibrations thudding through my chest.

One floor.

Two.

Three.

Why hadn't I eaten dinner last night?

Ninth floor. Eighth.

Thudding feet and the open-mouthed pants of everyone crowding the stairwell blended with the screech of the alarm. A long line formed, people moving as fast as they could, more joining us through banging doors at every landing. Vaguely I registered the second looks of numerous people as they recognized the band members. Their curious eyes made me want to shrink away.

Mick held me tightly by the right elbow, his other hand still poised above his gun.

Seventh floor.

Sixth.

Fifth.

My vision blurred, my feet moving on their own. I couldn't even feel them anymore. A buzzing started in my brain, whirling around and around, fueled with each sounding of the alarm. I dropped my jaw wide open, sucking air.

Fourth.

Third.

Almost there, Shaley, almost there.

Memories of the mall pierced my head. The noise, the crowd — I stumbled.

"Whoa!" Mick jerked me upright.

Second floor. Sweat rolled down my temple. I'd lost Brittany. Where was she?

One more level.

Ground floor. My heel banged down on the last stair.

I tripped on my own feet. Mick threw an arm around me and pulled me to the exit. We burst through the heavy door and into the parking lot. Cool air slapped my cheeks. I gasped.

A camera flash split the night.

The sudden light spun terror through me. I jerked back as if I'd been hit.

"Get out of here!" Mick roared. He encircled me with his arms, spun me away.

Another flash, a second, and third. I cringed in Mick's arms.

Then — pounding feet. They retreated into the night.

I squeezed my eyes shut and slumped against Mick's chest. Whimpers spilled from my lips.

"It's okay, it's okay." He patted my head. "They're gone."

Brittany and Mom ran up to us. Mom pulled me from Mick's arms and held me tightly. Soon the others materialized in groups, their chests heaving. Rich, Stan, Kim, and Morrey escorted by Wendell. Ross, Lois, Melissa, Carly, and Marshall with Bruce.

Inside the hotel, the alarm still screamed.

Mick scuttled us off to the side of the parking lot, away from other people and the bright pole lamps, and we formed a huddle.

The three bodyguards faced outward. Brittany and I clung to each other. Familiar voices spoke, cursing the alarm and lack of sleep — and how hard that would make the next concert. Mom and Ross talked in low tones. I couldn't say a word. Couldn't even get enough oxygen. I raked in air, tears biting my eyes. *Don't be such a baby*, I scolded myself. But too little sleep, no food, and way too much fear got the best of me.

My legs trembled.

The last thing I remember is sliding through Brittany's arms toward the hard, dark asphalt.

swam to consciousness, lying on my back. Brittany, Bruce, and Mom bent over me with distorted faces. I blinked hard. The left side of my head throbbed.

The hotel's fire alarm cut off mid-blare. The sudden silence roared in my ears.

"Shaley, can you hear me?" Mom sank down beside me, cradling me in her arms.

"Yeah, I'm ... My head hurts."

"You hit it when you fainted."

Ross stomped back and forth before our group, cursing. "Anybody see that photographer's face?"

Photographer. Flashes. The memories flooded back.

Vaguely I registered the negative answers.

"I didn't see it either," I whispered to Mom. "Everything happened so fast."

"I know, I know."

Ross whipped his cell phone from his pocket.

A hotel employee approached. "It's all right to go back inside now. Someone pulled a false alarm. We're so sorry."

Ross cursed again. "False alarm. Right." His narrowed eyes met Mom's. "This was *planned*."

She gave a tight nod.

Planned?

More memories swept over me. Mom not letting me go into the hall without me. Mick running with a hand near his gun.

Ross jabbed numbers on his phone.

The pavement felt so hard. I sat up straight. "I want ... I need to get up."

Mom helped me stand. "Feel all right now?"

Brittany peered at me with concern.

"Yeah. I'm okay."

"Detective Furlow, Ross Blanke here." His irritated voice boomed into the phone. "You need to get over here *right now*."

"Shaley, you okay?" Carly came over and hugged me. "Baby, I'm so sorry. I didn't even see you go down."

"It's okay. Really." I smiled crookedly. "Thanks."

"There is too much craziness going on here," Ross snapped. "I expect you to get to the bottom of it — *now*."

"Rayne," Mick said. "We should get back inside."

"Yeah. Okay." She pulled at Ross's arm.

"All right." He snapped his phone shut. "Detective's on his way." He looked around. "Let's go. Everyone stay together."

Mick, Bruce, and Wendell placed themselves on the outsides, the rest of us in the middle. Our thick group narrowed to enter the lobby door two at a time.

Ross halted. "Who's got room keys?"

Vaguely I remembered sticking mine in a pocket. I felt for it. "I do."

Some of our group hadn't remembered to grab theirs on the way out. Apparently neither had half the hotel residents. People were already streaming toward the reception counter. "All right, wait a minute. Raise your hand if you forgot your keys — one person to a room." Poking his finger in the air, Ross noted the hands. "Carly, Stan, Kim, Morrey. Okay, get on up to our floor. I'll bring your keys."

Heading toward the elevator, I glanced back to see Ross wedging himself at the front of the line.

Back in our room, I placed a small suitcase in the door to Mom's suite to hold it open. Brittany and I fell onto our beds and waited for Detective Furlow to arrive at Mom's room.

I still felt lightheaded. I really needed something substantial to eat, but nothing was available at the hotel at that hour. And our room's pay-as-you-eat bar with cookies and chips held no interest for me. My body craved protein.

Brittany turned toward me on her bed. "You thinking what I'm thinking?"

"You mean someone pulled that alarm to get us out of our rooms?"

"Not *us*, Shaley. *You*."

I blinked. "Why just me?"

"Come on. Who got the white rose and the photo? And *who* did that photographer take pictures of when we got downstairs?"

"You mean I was the only one?"

"Yup."

"You didn't see the person's face?"

"No. I wasn't even looking in that direction until the flashes went off. Then the light was too bright."

I stared at the ceiling. "Why go to all that trouble just to get another picture of me? Like they didn't get enough today."

"I don't know."

"Shaley." Mom appeared at the connecting door. "The detective's here."

I sighed and sat up. "You want to come, Brittany?"

"They probably won't want me in there. Leave the door open — maybe I'll be able to hear."

"Okay."

The detective looked rumpled as usual, but in a different wrinkled shirt and pants. A shock of his hair stuck out.

A still-agitated Ross joined us as we sat in the lounge area of Mom's room. He sat forward on one couch, knees apart and a fist against his hip. "That photographer was *planted*, I'm telling you. Mick, the bodyguard who was with Shaley, reported he saw no other signs of photos being taken until they ran out the door. Someone was waiting there for her."

"You get a look at the photographer?" The detective turned to me.

"No. The flashes were too bright, and I was too ..."

"She fainted about that time." Mom drew her bottom lip between her teeth.

Detective Furlow's eyebrows rose. "Are you all right?"

I leaned my head back against the armchair. "Yeah. I guess I hadn't eaten, and I was kind of wobbly."

"You had anything to eat yet?" His tone was gentle.

"No. We just got back into our rooms." I tried to smile. "You got here pretty fast."

"What do you want?" Ross stood up. "I'll call the front desk. They'll get something from the kitchen for you even if it is closed."

I hesitated, not wanting to put anybody out.

"Shaley," Mom said. "Order something or I'll order it for you."

My stomach twisted. Hungry as I felt, I wasn't even sure I could eat. "I don't know. Maybe a hamburger? Or a salad with chicken?"

Mom nodded. "Ross, sit down, I'll do this." She headed to the nightstand and picked up the phone. Turning her back to us, she spoke in a quiet but firm tone that said her daughter would not be denied.

Detective Furlow cleared his throat. "What happened to the photographer?" He looked from Ross to me.

I pulled my arms across my chest. "He ran away. Just snapped the pictures, then took off."

"Do you know for sure it was a man?"

I frowned. "No. Guess not."

Mom hung up the phone and returned to perch on the edge of her chair. "Food will be up soon."

"Thanks."

We exchanged tired smiles. It occurred to me that Mom had

paid me more attention in the last twenty-seven hours than she had in the many days before, all added together.

Detective Furlow focused on Mom. "At the end of our last meeting I told you we'd be questioning the photographers and reporters who showed up at the mall when Shaley was there. News footage has helped. We've been able to see for ourselves who was there. So far we've tracked down four people: The reporter for the *San Jose Mercury*; the photographer for *Shock*, Ed Whisk—"

"Vulture." Mom narrowed her eyes into slits. I made a face.

The detective tilted his head. "I can see where you'd get the name. Also we talked to Brenda Bloomenthal with the *All That's Hot* tabloid and a freelancer named Alan Crease."

Brenda Bloomenthal. We called her Frog. "What did the freelancer look like?"

"Big, overweight. Heavy jowls."

"Frodo," Mom and I said at the same time.

The detective smiled briefly. "All were questioned on camera at the station. All had alibis for the time of Tom's death, claiming they weren't even in town. Each one said he or she hurried to San Jose *after* the news broke about the murder. They all live in the Southern California area, so it wouldn't take long to hop a morning plane up here. But I've got people checking those alibis out."

"If that's true," Mom said slowly, "then none of them could have taken the photo that ended up in Shaley's shopping bag."

"That's right."

"What about the other photographers I saw at the mall?" I asked.

"Still tracking them down."

Detective Furlow's cell phone rang. He pulled it from the clip on his belt and checked the incoming number. His head came up. "Excuse me for a minute."

He held the phone to his ear. "Furlow."

His eyes roved over the room as he listened.

"Great. Good thinking. On my way."

He flipped the phone shut and stuck it back in his belt.

"Well." He looked from Ross to Mom. "We got a lucky break. Looks like one of our officers stopped a speeder not too far from the hotel. When he shined a flashlight into the vehicle, he spotted a large camera. The speeder's name is Len Torret. Said he works for *Cashing In*."

Len Torret. We called him Cat. The slinky, disgusting-looking man with bleached blond hair. Mom and I couldn't stand him.

The detective stood up. "The officer would have given Torret a ticket and let him go, but he got mouthy and refused to cooperate. So he was arrested. At the station, the officer heard talk of the fire alarm. I had checked in with the station after you called me." Detective Furlow nodded to Ross. "The officer put two and two together."

Cat. He'd been at the mall. Now it looked like he'd been the one in the parking lot tonight.

Had he put the "always watching" photo in my shopping bag?

As he started to leave, Detective Furlow shook hands with Ross. I watched their fingers clasp, and a sudden memory seared my brain. A memory of Tom ... and Cat.

My mouth dropped open. I turned wide eyes on the detective. "*Wait*."

Dark, chillingly empty streets of San Jose rolled by the window of Detective Furlow's car as we rode to the police station. The salad with chicken I'd ordered sat in a Styrofoam to-go box in my lap. I played with the plastic fork.

"Eat." Mom tapped the side of the container.

I forced a bite into my mouth.

We'd left Brittany in the hotel room. I hoped she was sleeping.

Ross sat in the passenger seat up front, unusually quiet.

Detective Furlow had been the one to suggest we watch him question Cat after I told him what I remembered. Things might go faster, he'd said, if we were there to prod him with information that came to mind during the interview.

Under any other circumstances, none of us would have chosen to stay up. We all needed sleep too badly, and tomorrow was a travel and concert day. Mom especially needed rest. Singing lead for Rayne was a *lot* of work — her voice had to be in tip-top shape, and the dancing required energy. Lack of sleep wreaked havoc on a voice. But the show had to go on — and go on it would. Mom would just have to rest as much as possible the following day.

Since Detective Furlow was with us — and he carried a gun — Mom hadn't pulled one of the bodyguards from bed. "Let them sleep," she'd said. "They'll need to be alert tomorrow, when the rest of us are dead on our feet."

I knew what she meant. All the same, I shivered at her use of the word *dead*.

"Here we are." The detective turned into a lit parking lot and stopped the car.

He led us into the station, passing the front desk and a few officers coming and going. "It's quiet here for a Saturday night," he remarked.

I followed mindlessly. If we went up or down stairs, turned right or left down halls — I have no memory. No way could I have retraced our steps on my own.

We ended up in front of a glass window in a small room. Along our side of the glass ran a rectangular table with three chairs. On the other side Cat sat in a second room of about the same size. That room looked grim and bare — except for its own battered square table and a couple of chairs. No pictures on the walls, nothing to make the place look comfortable or safe. I couldn't imagine being questioned in there by a policeman. It looked intimidating and frightening.

Although we couldn't see it, we were told a camera was mounted in the upper corner of the wall nearest us, pointed at the square table. At that table Cat slumped back in his chair, looking not one bit intimidated. More like annoyed enough to strangle somebody.

He was dressed in jeans and a blue, long-sleeved shirt with the cuffs rolled up. His white-blond hair looked ratty, and he had bags under his eyes. Cat was probably in his forties, but right now he looked more like sixty. He bounced a forefinger against the table, his other hand plastered to his hip.

His head turned, green eyes focusing on the window. Cat sneered right at me.

My head jerked back.

"It's okay." Detective Furlow pointed to the glass. "Remember, this is a one-way mirror. Looks like he can see you, but he can't."

My shoulders drew in. This man had hounded me today — at least once. And he may have done more than that. I didn't like standing mere feet from him, separated only by a window.

The detective gave us an encouraging smile. "Once I get in

there, if at any time you think of something important I should ask, tap on the door to the other room and then stand back in here. I'll come out, and we'll talk. All right?"

"Yes, thanks." Mom pulled in a deep breath and shook back her hair. Ross and I nodded.

"Okay." Detective Furlow pointed to the chairs. "Sit down if you like. We may be in there awhile."

He disappeared out our open door. A few seconds later we saw him enter the other room.

Mom, Ross, and I sank into the chairs.

Mom squeezed my leg. "Let's hope this gets us somewhere," she whispered. "And if Cat knows anything about the murder — I hope Detective Furlow gets him to spill his guts."

Me too.

I thought of Tom. Then remembered the black, bloody hole that had once been his eye.

Me too.

The anger had flamed into a crackling fire in his gut. Sleep would not come.

He gave up trying. He just lay there, staring up in the darkness at nothing. Shutting out all sound. The blackness above reminded him of another night, in a place far from this one, when he'd first talked to the person who'd sent him.

"Watch her on tour," the sender said.

"Why?"

The sender told him the reason. "And I'll pay you."

"You have the money for that? 'Cause if I do that, I'm not free to get a regular job."

"I have the money."

The memory ran vivid. He shifted positions on the bed. Laid an arm across his face.

That night had started it all. But at the time he'd never guessed where it would lead him. Where it would take his heart.

After a while he no longer cared about the money. He'd moved from just watching and reporting the actions of the Special One to protecting her. Because he loved her. Because she *needed* him.

Now she wasn't even grateful.

Such injustice. Such *denigration*. After all he'd done.

He would not stand back and take it.

Grunting, he turned over in his bed.

Tomorrow.

He opened his mouth, pulled in a deep, cleansing breath.

Tomorrow.

Hello, Mr. Torret. I'm Detective Furlow."

The detective's voice sounded pleasant and friendly. A tone, I thought, that was designed to make Cat trust him.

He held out his hand. Cat refused to shake it.

The detective dropped his arm and sat down on the opposite side of the table.

Cat reared back in his chair with a loud sigh, head flopping to one side. "About time you showed up. You got no right keeping me in here; I haven't done anything."

They regarded each other. Cat's eyes narrowed with suspicion.

The detective inhaled. "Before we start, I need to tell you that you have the right to remain silent. Anything you say can and will be used against you in a court of law. You have the right to an attorney. If you cannot afford an attorney, one will be provided for you." He raised his eyebrows. "Do you understand these rights?"

"Yeah, yeah, just get on with it. I want to get outta here."

The detective shifted his legs. "I hear you were speeding tonight when the officer stopped you."

Cat stuck his tongue under his upper lip and glared.

Detective Furlow drew the sides of his mouth down. "Almost seventy in a forty-five zone. That's pretty fast."

"No reason to take a person to jail."

"No, but interfering with the performance of a policeman's duty is. California Penal Code 69, in case you're interested. It's punishable by a fine of up to ten thousand dollars, up to a year's imprisonment, or both.

"I *didn't* 'interfere.'"

"That's not the way the officer saw it."

Cat shrugged.

"Why were you going so fast anyway?" Detective Furlow asked.

"I had places to go and people to meet."

"Man," Ross muttered. "We're not going to get a thing out of this guy."

"Which places, what people?" the detective asked.

"What difference does it make?" Cat's voice sharpened.

The detective let the nonanswer hang in the air. I wanted to slap Cat.

"I see you're from the L.A. area," Detective Furlow said. "What brought you to San Jose?"

"The Rayne concert."

"The concert? So you were there Friday night?"

"Yeah."

Mom and I gaped at each other. Cat was at the *concert.*

I thought back to our limo ride away from the arena. With all the flashes going off in the night, we hadn't been able to see the faces of any reporters or photographers.

Here was a member of the paparazzi who may have been at the mall, had been caught near our hotel tonight, *and* had been around when Tom was killed.

Cat had to be involved somehow. He *had* to.

But how could he have gotten backstage?

"Do you follow this group wherever the band goes?" the detective asked.

"No."

"What brought you to this particular concert then?"

Yeah, Cat — what?

He lifted a hand. "Rayne's been on the road three months. They went east through Texas and finally got back to the West

Coast. Since they were so near, *Cashing In*—the magazine I work for—sent me up. It's only an hour's flight."

Magazine, right. It was a tabloid.

Detective Furlow processed the answer. "Is that the only reason you came to the concert?"

"Yup."

I thought about the camera in their room. It would be recording everything Cat said.

Every lying word.

Detective Furlow leaned back casually and laced his fingers on his lap. "Okay. Let's move on for now and talk about where you were coming *from* when the officer stopped you. I think it was the hotel where Rayne is staying tonight."

"Really."

"In fact, I think you were in the parking lot when the band's members spilled out the door due to a false fire alarm. You took pictures of Shaley O'Connor."

Cat crossed his arms, chin tilting upward. He surveyed the ceiling as if it were a piece of art.

The detective bounced his clasped hands against the table. "We have your camera. Not a hard thing to review the photos on your memory card."

Cat's chin came down. His eyes shot daggers. "So *what* if I was at the hotel. It's my *job* to take pictures of celebrities."

"How did you know to be there when a fire alarm sounded?"

"I didn't. I just got lucky."

"After one o'clock in the morning—you just happened to be hanging out in the hotel parking lot?"

The hotel had security in its lot—I knew that. Cat couldn't have wandered around there long without being spotted.

He shrugged. "I'd been following them all day. That's nothing new for me. It's what I do for a living, and there's *no law against it*."

Mom made a disgusted sound in her throat. "There is if it turns into stalking."

The detective conveyed no reaction to Cat's attitude. "So tell me why you were there at one a.m."

"I already did."

He frowned. "I spoke to the two outside security guards at the hotel after the alarm. Neither of them remembered seeing anyone loitering in the parking lot. And they patrol on a regular basis."

"So I'm sneaky."

"Yes, I believe you are. Sneaky enough to stage that alarm to force everyone out of the hotel — so you could take pictures of Miss O'Connor."

Cat smirked. "You have a very vivid imagination."

"I wonder how vivid. You're telling me you just *happened* to be there at the perfect moment tonight, right? You got your exclusive pictures. You ran out of the parking lot and raced away — twenty-five miles over the speed limit. But you didn't have anything to do with the alarm."

He raised both hands, palms up. "You got it."

"And you also just *happened* to be at the very concert where a member of the Rayne tour was murdered."

"Guess I'm lucky that way."

My fingers curled around the arms of my chair. *Lucky* to have Tom murdered? I wanted to *strangle* Len Torret.

If Detective Furlow thought Cat's answer was despicable, he didn't show it. He rested his left elbow on the table, fingers digging into his cheek. "Just for the sake of argument, without that fire alarm, how would you have gotten your pictures of Shaley tonight?"

No answer.

He scratched his head. "Tell me, why are pictures of Miss O'Connor so important?"

Cat looked at him like he was an imbecile. "They're worth lots of money, that's why. Especially after the hair dresser got himself killed — and *she* found him. Every magazine in the country wants pictures of that band right now, and especially Shaley."

"So the murder, because it's a big news story, makes your photos of the band more valuable."

"Yeah."

The detective nodded thoughtfully. "And you say it was sheer 'luck' that you were at the concert when Tom was killed. None of your competitors were there — only you. When the band members drove away from the arena that night — once again, you got pictures."

Cat pressed back his thin shoulders, his head turning to one side. He gave the detective a look to kill out of the corner of his eye. "What you're insinuating is *insane*. You keep up that kind of talk, this friendly little conversation is over."

Ross shook his head. I knew what he was thinking — *this man knows far more than he's telling.*

Detective Furlow drummed his fingers on the table. "You were also at the mall this afternoon when Miss O'Connor was there."

"I was there because I'd had my feelers out about town, including the mall. Knowing the band had a day off, I figured one of them would show up somewhere. My diligence paid off. Apparently, my competitors had flocked into town after hearing about the murder. They all ended up at the mall too. So don't pin that one on me."

Cat ran his tongue between his lips and shifted in the chair. The detective said nothing, as if waiting for him to fill the silence.

"Besides, I've been doing some investigating of my own." A self-satisfied expression etched Cat's face. "Sounds like Shaley O'Connor was pretty close to this Tom guy."

Mom hissed. My hands flew to my mouth. For a moment I couldn't breathe. The media was hearing how Tom felt about me? What would they be saying on TV tomorrow? Would some reporter even manage to get into Tom's apartment and film his wall?

Sickness rolled around my stomach.

"Really?" The detective looked puzzled. "Where'd you hear that?"

Cat made a face. "I don't have to tell you."

I swallowed hard. Could he just be faking it?

But then how'd he *know*?

Ross ran a hand across his forehead. "Leaks," he said quietly. "It happens in police investigations all the time. Maybe he paid somebody on the force to talk."

Only then did I remember that Ross didn't know the full story. He hadn't heard about Tom's wall.

Detective Furlow cleared his throat. "Seems to me, Mr. Torret, if you wanted pictures of Shaley so badly, you'd go to some extra means to get them — like pulling a fire alarm."

Cat rolled his eyes. "Are we back to *that* again?"

The detective looked at him straight on. "*Did* you?"

"*No.*"

"He's *lying*," Mom said.

The detective let the answer hang in the air for a moment. "Let's talk about something else."

"How about the weather?" Cat smirked. "It was a lovely day yesterday, don't you think? And no rain predicted for today. But then, it rarely rains in northern California in the summer."

Impatience flicked across the detective's face, then was gone. He straightened his back. "You said you were at the concert Friday. Where were you exactly from ten to eleven o'clock?"

Cat's lips parted, and he stared, playing up his shock. "You're really *serious*? You think I killed that guy? I wasn't anywhere *near* him!"

"Look, we're asking everyone who was anywhere in the vicinity. If you had nothing to do with it, better to help us rule you out now."

"Fine. I was outside in the parking lot, as close as media was allowed to get. If you don't believe me, ask the local reporters and photographers who were there. Someone's bound to remember me."

Detective Furlow nodded. "I'll do that. But the question is — who *was* backstage that you were working with?"

"Huh?"

The detective rubbed a hand across the table. "You might not have killed Tom Hutchens yourself. But I think you paid someone else to do it."

"*What?* You're out of your mind!"

"Am I?" The detective leaned forward. "I know about your history with Tom. How you followed Rayne and Shaley O'Connor too closely one night last year. When Shaley got upset, Tom stepped in your face and shoved your camera away. You said — and I quote — 'You'll pay for this.'"

I frowned. Why was the detective pushing so hard all of a sudden? Wouldn't that make Cat just quit talking?

The photographer gave him a look. "So you think I had the guy killed. Just for that?"

"Not *just* for that. I think you also had him killed because you knew a murder on the Rayne tour would shoot the price of photos of the band sky high. And you figured after the way he defended Shaley, maybe he had a thing for her. All the more reason for pictures of her to rocket in price after his death."

Cat shoved to his feet. "You're *crazy*. I'm not — " He waved his hands in the air. "This conversation is *over*."

Detective Furlow remained seated. "Fine. It can be over anytime you want. Just know that I'm going to keep investigating you."

"You won't *find* anything!" Cat's eyes flashed.

"I wonder. Because I think it all ties in to the photo of Shaley you took in the hotel parking lot on Friday night. You know, the one with 'Always Watching' on the back that you dropped in her shopping bag at the mall?"

Cat stilled. He blinked rapidly, as if trying to pull himself together, then forced a smile. Slowly, with precise movements, he sat down. He leaned over the table as if talking to a stupid child. "Look. Mr. Detective. I don't know what your game is here, but you're wasting your time with me. Why don't you go find the *real* killer?"

Detective Furlow held Cat's gaze — for such a long time that Cat lost his cool. He leaned back, fingers fidgeting.

The detective cupped his jaw. "Do you know that a picture erased from a camera's memory card can be recovered by an experienced tech? Those cards are like computer hard drives. What's 'erased' isn't really erased."

Oh. *Oh.*

Like a jigsaw puzzle, the pieces of Detective Furlow's cunning game plan fell into place in my mind. He'd *purposely* pushed Cat too hard.

Cat gave a fake smile. "How fascinating."

"You know ..." The detective rubbed two knuckles beneath his chin. "When a person lies to me about one thing, it makes everything else he says suspect. Get what I mean?"

No response.

"So. If I have our lab tech look at your camera's erased pictures ... and he finds that 'Always Watching' photo you're acting like you know nothing about ..." He lifted both hands.

Perspiration shone on Cat's upper lip. He shifted in his chair, eyes lowering. One hand traced a forefinger along the table's edge.

A long, tense moment ticked by.

Cat sighed, then rearranged his expression into one of smug defiance. He raised his eyes to the detective and shrugged.

"Photography's my *job*. So *what* if I took that picture?"

My breath hitched.

"And you put it in Miss O'Connor's bag?" the detective pressed.

"Yeah. So what? No law against it."

"Not so sure about that. Why did you write the 'Always Watching' message on the back?"

"No reason."

Detective Furlow gave him a hard look. "No reason."

"Nope."

"And the reason you put the photo in her shopping bag?"

"Just for kicks."

The detective scratched his cheek. "You do some strange things for kicks, Mr. Torret. I thought you were all about making money. Why go to this trouble getting this message to Shaley O'Connor?"

No response.

"Well, I have an answer for you."

"Wonderful."

"As you admit, you're all about making money with your photos. Somehow you must have thought this would help you make money."

Cat smirked and looked away at the wall.

Bingo.

"If you don't want to talk about that, we can go back to Tom's murder."

"I *didn't* have anything to do with that."

For the next twenty minutes, Detective Furlow pressed Cat about the murder. But Cat refused to budge — he knew "nothing" about it. Neither did he know anything about the white rose I'd received.

"I'm not lying about either of those things!" Cat shouted.

The detective sat back, eyes locked on Cat's face.

Mom sighed. "The detective's not getting anywhere with this. Maybe Cat wasn't involved in the murder."

"But we can't know. Maybe he was working with someone else," Ross said. "Question is — are they just going to let him *go* in the meantime?"

Please no. I didn't want to be on the streets, knowing Cat could show up any minute. Or worse, be watching me unseen. The thought sent shivers down my spine.

The detective folded his arms. "I know you *are* lying about some things, Mr. Torret. You'd better tell me what you *did* do — and why. Or this could be a very long night."

Cat slumped in his chair, looking deflated and worn. "Okay, okay. I put the photo in her bag to scare her a little. No big deal."

To scare me? Righteous indignation kicked up my spine. Mom and Ross both uttered curses.

"Why would you want to scare her?"

Cat gave the detective another one of those you're-an-idiot looks. "Because if she's scared, she'll look more vulnerable. Those kinds of photos are worth more."

"I see." The detective cocked his head, as if pondering the logic. "So ... you scare her with the photo. Then later that night you pull the fire alarm. You figure when she runs out of the building, she'll *really* look tired and frightened by then."

Cat shrugged.

Shrugged.

No denial. He'd *done* it. He'd put me through all this just for some lousy pictures.

"Have I about summed it up?"

Cat looked around, annoyed. "Can I go now? You got what you wanted."

"Mr. Torret, *did* you pull that fire alarm?"

"Yes, yes! Okay? Now I'm done talking. You want more, get me a lawyer. Otherwise I'm out of here."

Slowly, Detective Furlow stood up, towering over Cat. "Hate to tell you, but you're not 'out of here.'"

Cat's face paled. "What?"

"As I see it, you got multiple charges. Tampering with a fire alarm is a misdemeanor in California."

"Yeah, a misdemeanor! Hardly a reason for you to keep me —"

"*And* you've violated California's anti-stalking law."

"I'm not a stalker!"

"Tell it to the judge. You sent Shaley O'Connor a message designed, by your own admission, to cause her to fear for her safety. And you pulled the alarm to further disturb her."

"Oh, come on!" Cat surged to his feet. "That's a twisting of the law if I ever heard it!"

Detective Furlow stared him down. "Like I said, tell it to the judge." He walked to the door.

"No, wait!"

The detective looked back, one hand on the knob. "An officer will be here in a minute to escort you to your cell."

Left alone in the room, the typically smug Cat crumbled into whining tears.

D etective Furlow finished questioning Len Torret at 3:45 a.m. As Mom, Ross, and I slid back into the detective's car to return to the hotel, my brain and body felt like they were wrapped in fuzz. As much as I'd wanted to concentrate during the last half hour of the interview, my eyes kept sinking shut. Still, it had been worth it to sacrifice our sleep. Especially watching Cat cry. Mom and I did a grim high five at that.

Detective Furlow's car smelled like ranch dressing and chicken. I'd left my salad on the seat.

"You should eat some more," Mom said.

I made a face. "It's icky and warm now."

As Detective Furlow started the engine, I sank back, my sluggish brain doggedly going over everything I'd just heard.

"You were great in there, Furlow," Ross said from the front passenger seat.

"Thanks."

Mom buckled her seat belt. "At least he's off the streets for a while."

"That was my goal. We needed to keep him behind bars as long as possible while we continue investigating the murder. I'm still not convinced he knows nothing about it."

Ross grunted. "Is he facing jail time over these current charges?"

"I *hope* so." Vengeance bittered my voice.

"Possibly." Detective Furlow pulled out of the station's parking lot onto the street. "The fire alarm tampering and the stalking charges each carry a maximum one year. But all his charges also carry fines, so it's possible a judge may only hand down that kind of sentence. For now, though, these multiple charges allow the prosecutor to ask for higher bail. Maybe that will help us keep him behind bars for a day or two."

My heavy eyelids closed. The vibration of the car was lulling me to sleep.

Mom heaved a sigh. "Can't you keep him because he's a suspect in a *murder*? Isn't that *enough*?"

"I wish it were that simple, but it's a stretch. We know he's been harassing Shaley. We know he was in town at the time of the murder. But we don't have anything concrete to tie him to that crime."

Anything concrete. That's what we still needed.

I massaged my forehead, dragging in deep breaths. I was beginning to wonder if I'd ever sleep again. Once in bed, would my brain even shut down? Plus I'd have maybe four hours before the alarm went off. I *had* to get up in time to eat something in the morning, or I was likely to faint in the airport.

Wouldn't *that* "vulnerable pose" put the paparazzi in a tizzy?

At the hotel, Detective Furlow escorted us inside and to our floor. He shook hands with each of us before leaving. We thanked him profusely.

He shrugged. "Just doing my job. And it's hardly done yet. Even though we won't be seeing each other, you can know I'll keep on this case. And I'll be in touch. I hope to have an answer about the white rose tomorrow."

Ross moved his wide neck from side to side, trying to work out the kinks. He had to tilt back his head to look the tall detective in the face. "And if Torret's lying about sending the rose?"

"Then I'll question him again. And next time I won't be so nice."

PART 3
Sunday

The buzzing alarm pounded nails in my head. I slapped it off and stared blearily at the closed curtains of the hotel room.

Brittany and I moved like slugs as we dressed, dreading our parting. Hopefully we could stay together until the last minute since she was flying on the same airline and our gates shouldn't be too far apart.

I so wanted to go home with Brittany. If only Mom had said yes.

I have to stay with you, Shaley, or there's danger ...

Brittany's expression told me she was thinking the same thing. Neither of us spoke it.

I was achingly tired, and my head felt pressed in a vise. I'd promised myself I would eat breakfast but now had no interest in food. My growling stomach stretched within me like a deep, black hole.

Our limos pulled away from the hotel shortly after ten a.m. Sitting next to Brittany, I closed my eyes and laid my head back against the seat. I felt miserable. At that moment I *hated* the tour. I hated the band. I just wanted to *go home*.

"You all right, Shaley?" Mom sat on the other side of Brittany, Kim next to her. Facing us on the opposite seat were Mick, Ross, and Morrey.

"No, thanks to you." My tone dripped with accusation.

Mom's voice edged. "I'm just trying to keep you safe, Shaley."

"I'd be safer away from this tour."

"You'll be safer where I can keep an eye on you. Not to mention the bodyguards."

Little good they'd done.

No one else spoke. Tension swirled around us all the way to the airport. I kept my eyes closed the entire ride.

The limo pulled to a halt.

"Heads up, Shaley, we're here." Mom sounded irritated. "And mind yourself if reporters show up. The last thing we need are news stories of you acting snotty."

Snotty?

Okay, so Mom was tired too. *Still, didn't I have a right to be angry?* I railed to myself. *How about Cat and the other paparazzi?* Not to mention the reporters. They were hounding *me*, remember?

Besides, at that moment I couldn't have cared less what *anyone* thought of me. Why couldn't everyone just leave me alone?

We entered the San Jose terminal, pulling our own bags, and headed for the upstairs level where check-in is located. Mom and I stepped off the elevator straight into a mass of reporters.

I shrank away. The reporters shouted, and TV cameras whirred. Flashes battered my eyes. Microphones were thrust toward me. I ducked and put a hand in front of my face.

"Rayne," some woman yelled, "what do you know about Tom Hutchens's murder?"

"Are there any suspects?"

"Shaley, is it true Tom was in love with you?"

The question stung like pelting hail. I reeled back.

"Shaley, talk to us!"

More reporters shoved. Cameras clicked on.

"Hey!" Ross shouted. "Get back and give us some room!"

"Shaley, was Tom your boyfriend?"

"Did the false alarm at your hotel have anything to do with the murder?"

"Were you dating anyone besides Tom?"

Wendell grabbed my arm. "Let's go."

My throat cinched shut. Brittany hung onto me. Keeping my head down, I watched the floor move under my stumbling feet. Bruce and Wendell closed in on either side of Mom.

Airport guards surrounded us as Ross checked our baggage. The questions and cameras wouldn't stop. I buried my head in Wendell's chest, hands over my ears, praying for Ross to *hurry*. Finally checked in, we were hustled through security as quickly as possible. Once we pushed into the lines, the reporters had to fall back.

Tears swam in my eyes as I walked through the security machine. On the other side, I could finally breathe.

Ross's face was red with anger. "Sorry about that, Shaley." He gave me a rough hug. "Those idiots don't even know what they're talking out."

Oh, yes they do. But how had they found out? Leaks from the police? The media now knew more about Tom's feelings for me than Ross and the band did. Wouldn't take long for Stan, Morrey, and all the rest to hear the sensational details. Then how could I *face* them?

Bruce, Wendell, and Mick formed a triangle around us as we headed to our gate. Reporters were gone, but fans and curiosity-seekers were everywhere. The band members always tried to be polite with fans, but this had been a rough couple of days for all of us. The looks on our bodyguards' faces sent the message—*leave them alone.*

"You okay, Brittany?" I reached for her arm. She could stay with me until we boarded.

"Yeah." She sounded as shaky as I felt.

At the gate, I fell into a chair, Kim on one side and Brittany on the other. Exhausted and sick at heart over Brittany's leaving, I stared at my lap.

Carly came over and patted my knee. "Want something to eat? There's a Starbucks nearby. I can bring you a sandwich."

I shook my head. "But thanks."

Brittany laced her fingers through mine. "Just stay close to your bodyguards — all the time. Everything'll be okay."

"But you said — "

"I know what I said."

"Then, what? That sense of yours telling you something new?"

She was silent for a moment. "You'll be okay. You *have* to be."

In other words — no.

An airline employee called for our boarding to begin.

Brittany and I stood up and clung to each other. Tears ran down her cheeks, wetting my own. "Take care of yourself. Be careful."

"I will. You're right — I'll be fine."

She pulled back. "Call me. A *lot*. The minute you get off the plane."

"I will." I pulled my top lip between my teeth. "I'm sorry, Brittany. I'm so sorry all this happened. I just wanted you to have a good time."

"No, it was the *right* time for me to be here. I mean, if this had to happen, I'm just glad I could be with you."

"Come on, Shaley." Mom touched my arm, empathy in her voice. "We have to go."

"Bye, Rayne." Brittany hugged my mom. "Thanks so much for inviting me."

"Sure. Wish you could have stayed."

Brittany stretched out her arm as I moved away, and we touched fingers until we could no longer reach.

Walking down the boarding ramp, I turned back for a final wave. She raised her hand with a sad smile.

A *month*. A solid month until I saw her again. The last two days themselves had seemed an eternity.

Mom's cell phone rang as we entered the plane. She pulled it from her purse, checked the ID, and answered in low tones.

I followed her into our first-class row — hers, the window seat, mine, the aisle. Sinking into my seat, I turned off my cell phone and shoved my purse under the chair in front of me. Mom was still talking to someone.

"I see." She stared blankly at the seat in front of her. "Well. That's really — " She laid her head back and gazed upwards. "Yes. We should. In fact she's right here. Would you tell her?"

She handed the cell to me, her expression serious. "Detective Furlow."

I tensed, searching her eyes. Now what? News about Tom's murderer I didn't want to hear? "Hi, this is Shaley."

"Hello. I understand you're on the plane. Glad I caught you. I just told your Mom we were able to trace the credit card buyer of that white rose you received."

It's my dad. The thought pierced me, an arrow through the back. I went weak. Maybe he really *was* out there trying to reach me. After all the years of wanting to find him, had it come down to this mundane moment, sitting on some stupid plane?

"Yeah?"

"Turns out it's not someone we'd thought of, but in hindsight, we should have guessed."

My heart knocked against my ribs. "Wh-who?"

"Tom Hutchens."

He awoke that morning to a bonfire in his belly.

In the few hours he'd slept, the flames of injustice had stoked themselves until their heat burned down every limb, every nerve.

He'd put his future on the line for Shaley O'Connor and received nothing in return.

He would set this despicable situation right. Today.

Pushing off his bed, he stumbled into the bathroom.

As he splashed his face, logistics played through his mind. Backstage at tonight's concert could pose problems. Would there be extra security in Denver after Friday's murder?

No matter. Such challenges would not deter a superior man like himself. Forget staging an "accident." Too much had happened now. He'd simply find a way to do what must be done.

Consumed by his vengeance, he ate breakfast alone. The eggs were tasteless and his coffee bitter.

When the fire is out, he thought. *When the fire is out, I can live again.*

Our plane sat on the tarmac for *two hours*. There was something wrong with a part, which had to be replaced and then checked. The pilot kept coming over the speakers, saying it would be "another half hour." That happened four times.

I should have slept through it all. I would have if Detective Furlow hadn't called with the news that shook my world all over again.

Tom had sent me the white rose.

The detective was right — we should have known. Hadn't we seen the photo of Tom's wall with all the dried white roses?

He ordered the flower Friday afternoon, just after we arrived in San Jose. A few hours later, he was dead.

On the airplane, as everyone fidgeted and complained about the delay, I stared at the back of the seat ahead of me. My mind reeled.

After we finally took off, Ross leaned halfway over the aisle to discuss logistics with Mom. Their conversation flowed in front of my face. With the late arrival, we wouldn't have time to go to our hotel first, he said. It would be straight to the Pepsi Center in downtown Denver. Even then, the band would be late for the usual four o'clock sound check.

Mom groaned. She was tired. She knew I was tired. She'd hoped to have a chance to rest — at least one hour.

"No way." Ross shook his head. "Just won't work."

"Well, obviously," Mom shot back. "You should have left us more than two hours' leeway. You know how late planes can be these days."

Ross cursed. "Gimme a break, Rayne. This is the first time it's happened on the entire tour."

"*Stop!*" I threw my hands up, casting a dirty look at them both. "Don't we have *enough* going on without you two fighting?"

Ross made a disapproving sound in his throat. Mom flung herself back against her seat, arms crossed. She snapped her head to focus out the window.

My eyes slipped shut, my thoughts returning to Tom.

I'm watching over you. The note he'd written with the rose. What had he planned after I received it Saturday? Was he going to tell me it was from him? Was he ready to admit how he felt about me?

What would I have *done*?

Sickness rolled around my stomach as I imagined the scene. I hated the fact that Tom was dead, of course I did. But a tiny part of me — a part I couldn't *stand* — was glad I didn't have to face him as he declared his feelings for me. That detestable part of my soul mired me in guilt, because it came all too close to relief that Tom was dead. I *wasn't* relieved. I *missed* Tom. Even if I would've had to listen to him say he loved me, even if I'd gotten mad at him for using a symbol so dear to me and Mom — even that confrontation would have been better than *this*.

Maybe he hadn't planned to tell me at all. Maybe he was going to listen to me tell him about receiving the rose — which I surely would have done — and see how I reacted.

I'm watching over you.

Not a message from my father. Silly, being disappointed over that. Hadn't I known the rose couldn't really be from him?

So why did I want to cry all over again?

A thought popped into my head. My breath caught. "Mom."

She turned from the window, eyebrows raised at the sudden intensity in my tone.

"Yesterday. Before we talked to Detective Furlow. You said we weren't the only ones who knew about the white rose. Obviously Tom knew. How? And who else knows?"

A rueful expression crimped her forehead. "Years ago, when Rayne was just beginning to go somewhere, I was interviewed by a magazine. They asked about your father. I didn't want to talk about that, so I diverted the conversation to something that had happened long ago between him and me. I told the white rose story. Who knows how many people read that and still remember? Today I wouldn't be surprised to find that interview on the Internet."

My jaw dropped. I'd dared believe only my father could have sent that rose. "Why didn't you *tell* me? I thought it was him!"

"I *told* you it wasn't. And then Detective Furlow came to the door and ... everything else happened."

Anger swirled around my chest. Why all this secrecy over the years? I was so tired of it.

I closed my burning eyes. Tears pushed out.

"Shaley." Mom's voice softened. "It's not bad news that Tom sent the rose. Now at least we know it has nothing to do with Cat's photo and message to you. Now the police can put the rose aside and concentrate on what matters."

My head nodded. "Yeah."

"Then don't be so downhearted."

I focused on my lap. Didn't she understand all the confusion I felt over Tom?

Mom looked out the window and let out a frustrated sigh. "I wish this *stupid plane* would get to Denver."

So much for worrying about me.

I couldn't stand the thought of facing another night backstage — without Tom or Brittany.

I folded my arms. "When we get to the Pepsi Center, I'm calling a limo to take me to the hotel. I want to go to *bed*."

She shot me a weary look. "You can't go alone."

"Then send Wendell with me. And Bruce. And Mick. And the

rest of the population for all I care. I'm not sitting backstage while you sing to your adoring fans."

Mom's jaw flinched. I'd hurt her. Guilt twinged my gut. What kind of terrible person was I turning into?

Her expression hardened. "Fine, then. You can go if you're going to be a brat. But I will have to send someone with you. Make that *two* people."

Flouncing back against the seat, I closed my eyes.

"Good. Whatever. *Who*ever."

I just want to hide from the world.

For about ten years.

40

Denver, the "mile-high city." Thousands of people were proud to call it home. To me it was just another town.

I called Brittany as soon as we touched down. She was already at her house.

"Miss you already," I said.

"Me too."

As soon as we left the airport's secure area — surprise, surprise — more reporters and photographers surrounded us. They hurled more stupid, humiliating questions at me, thrust more microphones in my face. Flanked by Wendell and Bruce, I pushed through the crowd, beyond tired and hating the band and everyone in it.

Our troupe scrambled into three limos.

"Hurry up!" Ross barked at our driver. "Get us to the Pepsi Center!"

Mom, Kim, Morrey, Rich, Carly, and Mick ended up in the car with me. As we raced through the streets, Ross tapped fingers on his knee, eyes flicking this way and that. Clearly he had a hundred things on his mind — all the concert details he'd have to check in a super hurry once we arrived at the arena.

No one spoke — until Mom's cell phone rang. She glanced at the ID, then at me, "It's Detective Furlow again." She flipped her phone open. "Hi, it's Rayne."

I leaned close to hear his voice through the cell.

182 —⁌ Brandilyn Collins and Amberly Collins

"I'm calling this time with not-so-good news," he said. "Len Torret is out on bail."

"Oh, no."

"I know. We just couldn't keep him. We still don't have enough evidence to connect him to Tom's death. However, he's been warned not to get within five hundred feet of Shaley or any of your band members."

Not enough evidence to connect Cat to the murder — that was an understatement. They didn't have *any* evidence. And Cat knew it. Even from five hundred feet, he'd find a way to flaunt that fact in my face. For all I knew he'd show up here in Denver.

Good thing I was headed for the hotel soon.

I focused out the window. Buildings and streets and men and women rushed by. Who were all those people, and why were they in such a hurry? I drew my arms across my chest. Lately the world loomed so big and noisy and frightening. Like some rickety wooden roller coaster rocketing through a black tunnel. You couldn't see what was coming next and didn't know what you'd do when it did come.

I just wanted to get off.

Someone is *always watching. That someone is Jesus.* Carly's words. *Were they only from yesterday?* They flashed into my brain and hung there.

Did I believe God watched the world?

I don't know. I guess.

Always watching. Every time those words ring in your head, Shaley, don't just think of the person in this world who wrote them. Think of God in heaven ...

A new sorrow welled up in me, deep and almost indefinable. I felt like a little girl searching desperately for something vitally important but not even sure what it was.

Good grief. I needed sleep.

I leaned back and shut my eyes. I tried to shut out the thoughts, but Carly's words glued themselves in my mind. The more I tried to fight them, the more they pulled at me.

Okay, Jesus. Are you watching me right now for real? If you are, could you help me through ... everything? Because I've had it.

41

The Pepsi Center is a pretty building with lots of glass. I remembered it from Rayne's previous tour. As we drove by I caught a flash of red, white, and blue flowers in the shape of a large Pepsi logo. Our limo pulled around the building and into the back parking lots reserved for performers.

The Rayne bus and the equipment trucks were parked in the back. Everything had been unloaded earlier that day. The crew was already inside with equipment set up, waiting for the band members to run the sound check.

Ross hit the deck running, no time to worry about getting me to the hotel. Since he carried the credit card and always checked us in, I'd have to wait until he could make a phone call to get me into my room without the card.

I snagged his shirt as he hurried by in the hallway. "Ross, let me go. *Please.* I can just put the room on my own card." My knees sagged, and my eyes wouldn't stay open.

Ross pulled out of my grip, barely slowing. "*No*, Shaley. I don't want to have to change all the accounting later. Just give me a minute."

A minute, right. More like five, ten, a half hour. I slumped on the ever-present blue sofa in Mom's dressing room, listening to snatches of songs and guitar riffs as Rayne went through sound checks. My stomach was so empty it felt tied in knots. Still, not one item on Mom's food table looked inviting. For some strange reason I longed for steak.

As soon as I got to my hotel room, I planned to order a thick sirloin.

Wendell and Bruce hung out in the room with me. "Don't leave her side," Mom had told them before trotting onstage.

I sank my elbow into the arm of the couch, a fist supporting my head. Memories of Tom clamped around my heart. If he were alive, he'd be with me right now, probably singing one of his crazy rap songs louder than anything onstage.

Brittany phoned, but I didn't want to say much, not with the two bodyguards in the room. And the call only made me more miserable. Brittany should have been with me.

With a sigh, I pushed to my feet. "I'm going to the bathroom."

Bruce and Wendell both got up to follow. I flicked a look at the ceiling. "You guys coming in with me too?"

As I came out of the bathroom into the hallway, Hawk, the stage manager, strode past, followed by our bus driver, Jerry. "Hey, Shaley." Hawk halted mid-step to hug me. He had to talk loudly over all the music. "How you doing? We've all been so worried about you."

"Me too." Jerry held a box in his hands. "How *are* you, Shaley?"

I managed a semblance of a smile. "Fine. Thanks."

Jerry smiled back. "I still need to tell you those stories to make you laugh."

"Yeah. I wish Brittany was still around to hear them."

"You mean she's gone?"

"Her mom made her go home. Too much happening."

"Oh." His expression saddened. "That's too bad."

Hawk looked at me intently.

Ross materialized out of his dressing room/office, obviously harried. "Okay. Shaley."

A flash memory hit me hard — Ross's previous dressing room, Tom on the floor …

"You're set for the hotel." Ross spoke rapidly. "Wendell and Bruce are going with you and checking into their own rooms."

"You sure they—" The music abruptly stopped. Sound check was over. My voice lowered. "You sure they both need to come? There could be a lot of reporters after the show. Mom will need two bodyguards with her. I'm just going to be in my hotel room."

"We'll be fine here." Ross pushed his long hair back, his huge diamond ring catching the light. "Bruce, call the limo. Soon as it comes you can get going."

"Yes, sir."

My shoulders sagged. "You mean a limo from the airport didn't wait outside?"

"No, I didn't know how long this would take. But one should be here soon after you call."

If I lived that long.

Voices yelled to each other from the stage area. Multiple footsteps sounded. Techs and band members spilled into the hallway, headed for dressing rooms, bathrooms, whatever. Stan, Rick, Morrey, Marshall, and sound tech Ed Husker all filed by, heads turning as they heard snatches of our conversation.

"I can drive you all in the bus if you want, Shaley. No big deal for me to drop you off and come right back." Jerry gestured to the box in his hands. "I just need to run this to the stage first."

I looked at Ross. He shrugged. "Fine with me."

Hawk's beady eyes jumped from me to Jerry to Wendell. "Here, Jerry, I'll take that." He reached for the box. "You go ahead."

"Thanks so much, Jerry." Limp with relief, I turned back toward Mom's dressing room before any of the men changed their minds. "I'll get my suitcase."

"No, I'll get it." Bruce shot me a smile as he turned away. He and Wendell were lucking out tonight, thanks to me. Much nicer to be in their own hotel rooms than hanging around backstage.

Good for them, better for me. Finally I was headed for a meal, some peace and quiet, and *sleep*.

42

They were going to the hotel.

His lips stretched in a slow, satisfied smile. Fate had intervened.

Still, it would be a challenge. He could leave no evidence pointing to himself. Quick work would be required.

He sucked air deep into his lungs. Flexed his fingers.

The fire in his gut burned.

Walking down the hall, he detailed logistics in his mind.

He stepped outside into the hot, hot Denver air, the anticipation of an imminent kill pumping through his veins.

Twenty minutes later, Jerry pulled our bus up to the hotel — an imposing black glass building in a pyramid shape. By that time I was totally wiped. As I lowered myself down the bus's stairs, the lack of sleep hit me like a two-ton brick. I stumbled on the last step. Wendell caught me. "Whoa there."

"Thanks."

Bellmen hustled to take our bags. When they were done, I managed a wave at Jerry. "Thanks so much!"

"No problem." He saluted and closed the bus door.

As we turned toward the entrance, he drove away.

I dragged into the nearly empty lobby, flanked by the two bodyguards, Bruce as tall and intimidating as Lurch, and Wendell as muscular as Atlas. *Good grief*, I thought. One look at these two guys and *nobody* would mess with me.

Wendell checked us in. The Rayne entourage would occupy the top floor, number sixteen. "Only your party will be on that level," the desk clerk said. His eyes lingered on me as he handed over the slide-in cards — a look that pulsed with knowledge from news reports. "It's quiet here tonight. We just had a big convention pull out of town this afternoon. Enjoy your stay."

"Thank you."

Quiet I could handle.

Bruce had been assigned a room right across the hall from my suite, and Wendell's room was two doors down from mine.

Later, when everyone else showed up, they'd both be getting room-mates, but until then they could enjoy some rare privacy.

In the elevator I sagged against the wall, eyes closed.

When we reached my room — last one before turning the corner to the stairwell — Wendell checked it out, including the bathroom. The bellman glanced at Wendell curiously, then pulled my suit-cases over to the bed. I tipped him, and he left.

"All right." Bruce pointed his thick finger at me, his face in a stark, angular frown. "You're not going anywhere, understand? Not without calling us."

"Don't worry. I'm not leaving this room. I just want something to eat and to go to bed. You two rent movies on TV and enjoy the evening."

Wendell smiled, light catching the shiny surface of the scar on his chin. "I'm planning on it."

Bruce stroked his goatee. "I might go down to the restaurant. So call my cell phone if you need me, not the room number."

"Gotcha."

They stepped into the hallway. Bruce looked back. "Bolt your door."

"I *know*, Bruce. Now go *away*."

For emphasis, I shut the door in their faces. *Click* went the bolt. *There*. Now maybe they'd be satisfied.

I staggered to the bed and fell on it, not even bothering to take off my flip-flops. In a jeans pocket, my cell phone dug into my back. I leaned to one side, slid it out, and laid it on the nightstand.

Across from me on a table I noticed the binder that would con-tain the room service menu. *Sigh*. It seemed so very far away. I'd get it ... in a few ... minutes.

My drooping eyes closed ...

A heavy thud sounded from the hall.

My eyelids hinged open.

What was that?

I lifted my head from the pillow, listening.

Nothing.

Bruce? Wendell?

A groan.

My breath stopped. Had I really heard that?

"Sha-ley." A low voice, thick, dragged out. Like someone calling for help.

Was I dreaming?

I sat up, pushed off the bed. My limbs and chest felt drugged, blood moving like sludge through my veins. Part of me wasn't even sure what I was doing.

My feet stumbled across the carpet to the door. I pressed my ear against the wood, fingers splayed and tensed.

Another groan.

Bruce.

Heart leaping to my throat, I fumbled with the bolt, shoved it back. Cautiously, I opened the door.

He lay on his back in the middle of the floor near the corner. One leg drawn up, left hand to his huge chest.

Red seeped through his fingers, bubbled from his mouth.

"Bruce!" I blurted his name and ran to sink onto my knees beside him. "Wh-what happened?"

His face crumbled with pain, eyes squeezing shut. Jaw wide open, he dragged in air. It gurgled in his windpipe.

The world blurred. "Bruce, *please*. Don't — "

I pushed the bloody hand off his chest, smearing my own fingers. A red and black bullet hole pierced his shirt near his heart.

No.

Dizziness swept over me. I swayed, catching myself with a fist against the floor.

Wendell. I needed to get him. He had to *help*.

I pushed up, trying to rise.

Bruce's red-stained fingers clamped around my wrist.

Air backed up in my throat.

Bruce's eyes opened. His head turned, bleary gaze searching for my face. "H-he ..." Breath backfired in his chest. His back stiffened, arched off the floor, then back down. "He s-said ..."

A sob spilled out of my mouth. "What, Bruce? Who?"

His hand fell from my arm. I saw his eyes flatten, life draining away like ocean water through sand. With all his might, he struggled to move his lips. They came halfway together, trying to form a name. His throat jerked in a swallow.

"Just hang on! I need to get my phone, call 9 – 1 – 1."

"Nn — " The sound vibrated from his throat. Blood bubbled out of his mouth.

I dug my fingers into the carpet, leaving an imprint of blood. *Oh, no, Shaley, don't faint. Get up, get your cell!*

Bruce's right arm rose from the floor. With a shaking hand he pointed down the hall. "W — "

He trembled violently, and his hand thumped back to the carpet. His face relaxed. His head flopped over, eyes looking straight at me. Glazed, seeing nothing.

"No, Bruce, no!" I wailed. I rocked his body. He didn't stir.

Grief and panic descended, suffocating me. Bruce had been *shot.*

The killer's here.

Somehow I pushed to my feet, staggered down the hall toward Wendell's room. I could barely breathe, barely *think.*

Five feet from his door, it hit me. *W —.* Bruce had tried to say his name. Had pointed toward his room.

No. Not Wendell.

Yes, Wendell. Otherwise he'd be out here. I'd heard something; why hadn't *he?*

Mind whirling, I lurched away on stiff legs. Refusing to look at Bruce's body. *Get to your room, lock the bolt. Call for help!*

I rammed into my door, one hand fumbling with the handle. Blood smeared onto the gold metal.

Locked.

My shoulders sagged. Of course. It locked automatically. And my key was inside.

Bruce's cell. It should be clipped to his waist.

My head turned, eyes taking in his body, the red on his chest and face and hand. I would have to touch him, move his heavy torso to get to the cell holder at his side.

A force beyond myself swiveled me toward him. As I reached him, I turned away from his face. Not for anything could I look into those flat, open eyes.

I bent over, held my breath. Reached sticky, trembling fingers toward his side.

A sudden sound nearby — a bolt sliding back.

I jerked around. Which room had it come from? Wendell's?

No time to gamble. I shoved to my feet and ran.

heaved myself around the corner and out of sight. No time to think, no time to plan. *Just get out of here!*

I reached the stairwell door and forced myself to stop. My hand reached for the knob and turned it soundlessly.

From around the corner, I heard the click of a door opening.

Praying the hinges wouldn't creak, I pulled back the stairwell door. It was heavy. I slipped through the crack, feeling sweat bead on my forehead. I flattened my palm against the other side and slowly, carefully eased the door shut.

It closed with a light metallic sound.

Had Wendell heard?

Get out of here, Shaley!

My feet scurried to the stairs. I stopped, slipped off my flip-flops and clutched them in my left hand. Gripping the cold iron rail, I hurried down the steps as quietly as possible.

At the next landing, I stopped to listen.

I knew every noise would echo up the stairwell. I looked down and saw one dizzying flight after another. If Wendell opened that door one floor above me, I'd never outrun him.

Blood whooshed in my ears. Above me — silence.

Wendell was probably at Bruce's body by now. Did he plan to move it somehow? Dispose of it? Then what — come looking for me?

He'd think I was in my room. Until I didn't answer his knock —

The smear of blood of my door! Wendell would know I'd been out in the hall, seen Bruce's body . . .

With a small cry, I flung myself down two more flights. Breathless, I skidded to a halt and cocked my head. Was he following now?

Above me, a door clacked.

I flattened myself against the wall next to the exit. Floor Twelve, the painted sign on the door read. Like many hotels, this one didn't have a thirteenth floor.

"Shaley!" Wendell's voice bounced around the stairwell.

I yanked open the exit and tore into the hall.

The door slammed shut behind me. No going back now. He'd *know.*

I sprinted around the corner, praying to see someone, but the hall was empty. Where should I go? What should I do? The only way out was the elevator on the other side. Even if I got there, would I have time to wait for it?

Blood pounded in my ears as I ran. Halfway down the long corridor, I saw another hallway opening up to the right. I knew it would lead only to other rooms. I passed it without slowing.

At the end of the hall, I tore around the next corner. Nothing there but the elevator. Frantically I pushed the down button. My head jerked up, eyes searching for the red digital numbers that told what floor the nearest car was on.

Sixteen.

Maybe I'd make it.

Air heaved from me in gasps, my heartbeats an earthquake in my chest. I flung terrorized glances toward the corner, expecting Wendell to materialize any minute.

Fifteen. The elevator hung there.

My legs shook. I smacked the down button again and again, praying for the elevator to *move.* Surely Wendell was coming down the stairwell. Would he check each level? How long before he found me?

Fourteen.

The elevator stopped once more.

"Come on, come on." One more floor, just *one more —*

From the other end of the corridor, a metal door opened. Slammed shut. "Shaley? Shaley!

He couldn't see me, not yet. But the way he ran, it would only take him a minute to sprint the length of the corridor.

My eyes glued to the floor number above the elevator. *Please, please.*

Twelve.

The door slid open. Jerry Brand was inside.

He jumped out and grabbed me, pulled me into the elevator. My flip-flops slipped from my hand.

"*What*?" Automatically I fought, shock stinging my nerves.

"Shhh!" He smacked a floor button and pushed me toward the back of the elevator. With a wild look over his shoulder, he searched the hallway. No sign of Wendell.

Jerry flattened himself against the side wall, body taut with tension.

The elevator door panels started to slide shut.

Wendell careened around the corner. Our eyes met.

"Shaley!"

He hurled himself toward me. His face was flushed, danger in his eyes. Both hands were bloody.

"No!"

I melted against the wall.

As he reached the door, the last few inches of space between us closed.

The elevator surged downward.

Jerry sagged with relief. My knees turned to water. I pushed my hands to my temples and slid down the wall into a crouch.

"It's all right, Shaley. We made it."

Head down, I stared at the floor between my bare feet, breath huffing. "What are you ... doing here?"

"I drove away, then came back. Something just felt ... off."

Brittany. Jerry must have the same intuitive sense. And she'd been *right.* If she were with me right now, if there were two of us together, Wendell probably wouldn't have tried this.

The elevator went down, down. It seemed like the longest ride I'd ever taken. "Did you hit the lobby button?"

"No, the lowest level."

"Why?"

"He'll expect us to stop at the lobby."

"But we'll find people there, someone to help — "

"He has a *gun*, Shaley. He can shoot distances."

"You think he'll do that in a crowd?"

Jerry's voice dropped low. "Would you have thought he'd kill Tom and Bruce?"

I stared at the floor. No. I wouldn't.

Bruce is dead. I envisioned the blood gurgling from his mouth, his struggles to warn me. He was dead because of *me.*

"Shaley." Jerry put his hand beneath my arm. "You need to be ready to run as soon as the doors open."

As he helped me up, I seared him with a look. "Why is Wendell doing this?"

"I don't know."

The elevator stopped. Its doors parted to reveal a huge, empty hall carpeted in a design of blue and gold circles. No people.

"Come on." Jerry clamped his fingers around my arm and pulled. We ran.

"Where ... are we ... going?" I puffed.

"Out a lower exit ... and upstairs onto a back street. The bus ... is there."

We sped past an entrance to a large meeting room. In peripheral vision I glimpsed chairs set in rows, a podium up front. My heart wanted to split out of my chest. This level was so huge and long, and the exit so far away.

What about Wendell? If Jerry and I reached safety, Wendell might disappear before we could call the police. How could I step foot onto any street, knowing he might be out there waiting for me?

A series of smaller doors appeared on our right, more closely spaced.

Behind us in the distance — the *ping* of an elevator arriving.

"Go, go, go!" Jerry pulled me harder.

"You're not going to get away from me!" Wendell yelled.

Jerry cursed. "In here." He shoved me through the first door.

We tumbled into dimness.

I hit the floor, breath knocked out of my lungs. Jerry half tripped over me, regained his balance, and lunged up. He smacked on an overhead light and slammed the door closed, fingers fumbling with the latch. "There's no lock."

Breathing hard, he cast desperate looks around. We were in a supply room with a tile floor and no window. Two walls of shelves contained glasses and utensils and white cups, tall silver coffee urns, towels and cleaning solutions, a rolling table and projector. Against a third wall were a few chairs and a small sofa.

Jerry grabbed a chair and wedged it under the door handle. "Help me with the couch."

We leapt to either side of it and shoved it across the room and up against the chair.

I cringed back from the door, a hand to my mouth. Nothing left to do, nowhere to run. We were trapped, and our makeshift barrier wouldn't hold long.

My legs shook. "Do you have your cell phone?"

"No." Jerry's voice held quiet desperation.

"Then what are we supposed to *do*?"

Slowly, he turned to me. In his eyes burned a manic mix of accusation, hatred, and pain. "This is your fault."

I stared at him.

"I would have saved you. Protected you. I *did* protect you. But you've shown not one *ounce* of gratitude."

"What —"

Something heavy thudded against the door. I jumped.

"Move to the back wall, Shaley." Jerry yanked up his T-shirt and slid a gun from the waistband of his pants.

My eyes rounded. "You have a —"

"Move!"

Another thud. "Jerry!" Wendell's muffled voice.

Jerry pushed me backward, his expression blackened, his lip curled. "First, I took care of that makeup artist." He sneered. "Tom, with all those pictures of you on his wall. We were friends — until he told me about those pictures, how he loved you."

The *anger* on Jerry's face. He'd become a person I didn't even know.

"And Bruce. I saw what he did. On TV, in front of everyone."

"Wh-what?"

Jerry's eyes narrowed. "In the mall. He threw his arm around you, pressed his body close."

"He was *protecting* me."

"Bodyguards have no *right* to touch you," Jerry hissed. "*I was your protector." He jabbed a finger against his chest. "I put my life on the line to get rid of Tom. And all you did was cry and moan and go *shopping*! I thought you were worthy of me. You're *not*!"

The truth spun through me, turning my blood to water. Wendell, calling my name, chasing me. To keep me safe when he saw Bruce had been shot? Wendell, with blood on his hands. From kneeling over Bruce's body, checking to see if he was dead?

A hard kick hit the other side of the door. The chair rattled.

Jerry's arm shot around my neck.

I pummeled him with my one free fist. "Let me go!"

"Shut up!" He pressed the gun against my temple.

I stilled. Terrible, long seconds passed.

"What do you *want* from me?" I whispered.

"What I *wanted* was some gratitude. Now it's too late."

Was this man *insane*?

"How could I have shown you I was grateful? I didn't know it was *you*."

"You should have known, Shaley. You *should* have understood."

A second kick against the door. The chair and couch sputtered forward against the tile. The door wedged open an inch.

"Jerry!" Wendell's voice sounded hoarse with adrenaline and fear.

"Wendell!" I screamed. "Help!"

Jerry's arm tightened around me. "You come in here, I shoot her!"

My vision blurred. "Jerry, stop, *please*. I'll do whatever you want."

"I want you to *care* for me."

"I *do* care. *A lot*."

Keep talking, Shaley, just tell him what he wants to hear.

"I *know* you've tried to protect me. I didn't like the way Bruce touched me either. And Tom — I didn't even *know* how he felt about me."

"Jerry." Wendell's voice spoke through the crack in the door, as if his mouth was right against it. "Let her go and open up. You won't be hurt."

"Shut up, Wendell! I'm *not* coming out!"

My fingers curled toward my palms. This man was going to kill me. "Please listen to him. I don't want you hurt."

"Nobody else is gonna hurt me. *Ever again.*"

I swallowed hard. "I'll go with you somewhere. Is that what you want? I'll tell him I want to go."

"He'd never let you."

"Jerry Brand." Another man's voice outside the door. Calm, collected. "This is Sergeant Stratton with the Denver Police Department. I'd like to talk to you. Just let Shaley come on out, and we'll talk."

Jerry yanked me two steps to the left. The gun dug into my head.

"No!" Tears bit my eyes.

"Get out of here!" Jerry yelled. "All of you. Or she's dead."

"J-Jerry, *please.*"

He put his lips close to my ear, breathing hard. "We won't get out of this alive."

"They'll let us live. Just open the door."

"Soon as I do, they shoot me."

"No they won't. And I'll go with you — wherever you want."

"You think I'm *stupid*, Shaley? Think I believe you after the way you've treated me?"

The gun twitched against my temple. Jerry was losing it. Any minute now he'd pull the trigger.

I squeezed my eyes shut and made my only choice. "Hey, out there! Promise you won't hurt Jerry, and we'll come out!"

"That's fine." The sergeant's voice remained cool. "We're standing back."

My foot tried to move forward.

"Stop." Jerry held on tight.

I reached deep inside me for every ounce of courage I could

find. "We're going or I start screaming. And if I do, they'll break through that door in seconds."

"No."

Fine then.

My legs wobbled.

"Oh." I staggered against him. "I'm … getting … dizzy."

Abruptly, I went limp.

My sudden dead weight pulled him downward. He struggled to hold onto me as I sank toward the floor. The gun barrel slipped from my head.

Still I feigned unconsciousness. I sagged lower, Jerry's one arm not possessing the strength to stop me.

He uttered a curse. I heard the gun hit the floor.

I slipped to the tile face down, wrenched over, and kicked the gun toward the door.

"Help!" I screamed. "Get in here!"

Jerry bounded up, headed for the weapon. I grabbed one of his ankles. He stumbled to his knees.

"Wendell! Help!"

Heavy thuds hit the door. The couch and chair legs screeched against tile as the opening widened.

Jerry shook off my grip and crab-walked toward the gun.

"No!" I crawled after him, grabbing for his foot.

More battering at the door. It shoved open, the couch surging forward and over the gun. Jerry dropped to his chest, fished under the sofa and yanked it out.

A policeman burst into the room, both hands clutching a gun. "Freeze!"

Jerry pushed to his knees and brought up his weapon.

The policeman fired a deafening blast. Jerry listed over onto his side.

"Aaah!" I scrambled away and fell, hands over my ears.

"He's down!" The policeman ran to Jerry and snatched up his gun.

Wendell barreled through the door. "Shaley!"

"H-here." I struggled onto my knees.

Jerry groaned. The policeman turned him onto his back, his chest red. *Like Bruce.*

He wasn't going to make it.

Something within me pushed me toward Jerry.

"Shaley, stay back." Wendell reached down for my arm, but I waved him away.

"I have to ... know ..." I shuffled on my knees to the man who had been my friend, who'd told funny stories to make me laugh.

The policeman trained his gun on Jerry. Two more officers spilled through the door.

Jerry's mouth twisted in pain, his eyelids flickering. Air wheezed in and out of his throat.

He looked at me through dazed eyes.

I stared back, wanting to speak, but only able to watch him fight a losing battle for his life. He'd killed Tom and Bruce, had threatened to kill me. Still, grief for him poured over me. It had all happened so fast, I couldn't yet grasp it. What *happened* to this man?

"Jerry. *Why?*"

He blinked hard, trying to focus. "Come ... close. Have to ... tell you something."

"No, Shaley," Sergeant Stratton commanded.

I ignored him. What could Jerry do to me now? He was *dying.*

Holding my breath, I leaned down so he could whisper. Whatever he had to say, I wanted no one else to hear.

Jerry's lips moved in the tiniest of smiles. His eyes cleared and warmed, turning him back into the man I had known. For that one second — the second that would change my life — he looked straight into my soul.

"Your father sent me."

46

Officers swarmed into the supply room. Voices and radio static filled my head. My mind and body were beyond numb.

Wendell helped me to my feet and out to the huge hallway.

I hugged him hard, feeling the rock solidness of his muscles. "I'm so sorry I ran from you. I thought ..."

"I know." He tried to smile. "I look like a bad guy. What can I say?"

So much commotion around me. I started to shake. The hotel manager ushered me and Wendell into his office, away from the noise. I sank down on a small couch and stared at my bare feet.

Wendell left and returned with my flip-flops.

A female officer, fearing I was near fainting, brought me a yogurt smoothie. I managed to drink half of it.

When my mind cleared enough to think a little, I asked if I could use the manager's phone. I called Brittany and told her what happened. Except for one very important detail.

Someone phoned Mom, and she came racing over with Mick. Didn't even wait for a limo, just demanded that some local stagehand drive them. By the time she arrived, it was six p.m. The concert was supposed to start at eight with the warm-up band. Rayne was taking the stage at nine.

Mom rushed into the manager's office and swept me into her arms. "Shaley, Shaley!" She stroked my hair. "I'm so glad you're all right. I don't know what I'd do without you."

We held each other and cried until our tears ran out.

"You have to go and get ready," I told her. "The concert ..."

"I don't *care* about the concert. I'm not leaving you."

We sat in silence, fingers laced.

Your father sent me. Inside me the words thrashed and rolled.

I wiped tears from my face. My head throbbed. "I miss Bruce and Tom. I can't believe they're dead."

I missed Jerry too. The Jerry I used to know.

Mom pulled in a deep breath. "I can't believe any of this either." She squeezed my leg. "But it's over now. It's all over."

No, it wasn't.

Your father sent me.

Twice I almost told her Jerry's dying words. But I couldn't.

Of course I should have. She should know, as well as the police. But the words burrowed too deep down inside me. I couldn't bring them to my mouth, much less hear myself utter them. Shame, rage, confusion, grief ... all those emotions kicked through my chest as I clung to my mother. Part of me wanted to shake her for her secrets. But I could feel her deep love for me, and the anger wouldn't stick. Because, no matter what, I needed her so very much.

Besides, what if Jerry wasn't even telling the truth? He'd obviously been thinking crazy things. In his warped way of "protecting" me, did he think the best last words he could say were to give me hope about my father?

But how did he even know I *wanted* that hope?

Anyway, why should Jerry think his words were good news? My father sent a *killer* into my life. Wonderful. Did the man hate me?

At 6:30 Mom's cell phone rang. I could hear Ross's voice as they talked. He was worried about me. She told him I was okay.

"Look, Rayne," he said, "I have to make a decision by seven thirty whether we have a concert tonight."

"Okay. Whatever." Mom rubbed a hand across her forehead. "I just know I'm not leaving Shaley."

A plainclothes detective came and questioned me. He was a small man, gray-haired and craggy-faced. Looked like he'd seen a lot of hard things in life. I told him everything I could remember — except for Jerry's last words. Apparently Wendell or the police officer had reported that Jerry whispered something to me in his final moments.

"What did he say?" The detective asked.

Mom's hand on my arm felt protective and warm. I looked into her eyes. They glistened with love for me.

Lowering my gaze, I shook my head. "Nothing important."

Shortly after seven, the interview was over.

The detective stood. "Thank you, Shaley. You're a very brave young lady."

Brave? I almost laughed.

Mom put her arm around my shoulder. "Finally, you can go to your room and rest. I'll stay with you. With Wendell and Mick posted outside the door."

I shook my head. "You've got a concert tonight."

"We'll cancel it, Shaley. I'm not leaving you."

"You won't have to. I'll be backstage, listening to every song."

Her mouth opened, then closed. She pushed a strand of hair off my cheek. "I couldn't sing tonight even if I wanted to. Not after almost losing you."

My lips curved. "Of course you can. You're Rayne O'Connor. And Rayne reigns."

She managed a wan smile. "Thanks. But really — "

"Really, you *will*." I took her hand. "Come on. Let's get to the arena."

47

Rayne, you reign! Rayne, you reign!"

At nine p.m. in Denver's Pepsi Center, I sat backstage, too exhausted to be on my feet, chanting with the sold-out audience. Pride for my mom swelled in my chest.

She and the band members filed past me, ready to go onstage. I held up a palm. Mom and I high-fived.

"Go get 'em!" I shouted.

She grinned. I could see the adrenaline rush in her cheeks, feel the energy pulsing from her body. Despite her own tiredness and grief, she would give her fans the show they'd come to see.

Carly stopped to hug me. "Love you, Shaley!"

"Love you too."

She placed her hands on my cheeks. "Thank God you're safe."

I smiled. "He's 'always watching,' right?"

Joy flicked over her face. "Yes, he is!"

Laser lights kicked on, whisking over the stadium in red, blue, and white. The crowd screamed.

The band and backup singers ran onstage. Mom's glittery blue top shimmered in the spotlights.

He's always watching.

Funny how the words resonated within me. I'd said them merely for Carly's sake. But after all I'd just lived through, I wanted to *believe* them.

Are they true, God?

Stan strummed a hard minor chord on his lead guitar, and Mom's voice filled the stadium.

> I was made for you, and you for me,
> To walk a path together, our life's destiny.
> But time shattered our road, pulled us apart.
> You left me stranded with half of my heart . . .

I'd heard the lyrics hundreds of times, but suddenly they seared me. I brought laced fingers to my lips and stared at Mom.

Was this song about my dad?

Your father sent me.

I pictured Jerry's paling face. Were the last words he'd spoken on earth lies?

If not, *why* had he been sent? Was my father such a terrible man that he'd want a killer close to me and Mom?

A burning desire surged through my veins, one that I knew would not, *could not*, leave me. The desire to *know.*

> Tell me, tell me, where else to go?
> Tell me, tell me, was it all for show?

Rayne O'Connor strode across the stage, thrust her hand in the air.

Mom. I would have to tell her what Jerry said. And she would have to tell me her secrets. Without that knowledge, I'd never understand any of this.

That would be a painful, hard conversation.

Can you help us, God?

> I'm here, you're gone, what's left of my life?
> Sadness, confusion. Memories. Strife.
> Do you know? Do you care? Can you see me here?
> Which turn to take? The path isn't clear . . .

The song reached its final chorus. Mom held the last note long and clear as the guitars riffed, the drums thumping in my chest. With a crash of cymbals, the music ended. Thousands of fans clapped and whistled and cheered. I joined in.

Somehow amidst all the noise, Mom must have *felt* my applause. For at that moment she turned to me and smiled.

As another song blasted through the arena, I made a vow to myself. For me, for Mom.

I would seek the truth — until I knew it all.

the Rayne Tour

LAST
BREATH

BRANDILYN COLLINS
& AMBERLY COLLINS

Read chapter 1 of *Last Breath,*
Book 2 in The Rayne Tour.

Your father sent me.

The last words of a dying man, whispered in my ear.

Were they true? What did they mean?

Guitars blasted the last chord of Rayne's hit song, "Ever Alone," as Mom's voice echoed through the Pepsi Center in Denver. The heavy drumbeat thumped in my chest. With a final smash of cymbals, the rock song ended. Multicolored laser lights swept the stadium. Time for intermission.

Wild shrieks from thousands of fans rang in my ears.

I rose from my chair backstage. Tiredly, I smiled at the famous Rayne O'Connor as she strode toward me on high red heels. In the lights her sequined top shimmered and her blonde hair shone. She walked like a rock star — until she stepped from her fans' sight. Then her posture slumped. Mom's intense blue eyes usually gleamed with the excitement of performing, but now I saw only sadness and exhaustion. How she'd managed to perform tonight, I'd never know. Except that she's strong. A real fighter.

Me? I had to keep fighting too, even if my legs still trembled and I'd probably have nightmares for weeks.

Your father sent me.

I had to find out what those words meant.

"You're a very brave young lady," a Denver detective had told me just a few hours ago. I didn't feel brave then or now.

"You okay, Shaley?" Mom had to shout over the screams as she hugged me.

I nodded against her shoulder, hanging on tightly until she pulled back.

The crowd's applause died down. Voices and footsteps filled the stadium as thousands of people headed for concessions and bathrooms during the break.

Kim, the band's alto singer, laid a tanned hand on my head. A white-blonde strand of hair stuck to the gloss on her pink lips. She brushed it away. "How you doin'?

"Fine."

Bodyguards Mick and Wendell walked over to escort Mom. Wendell's eyes were clouded, and his short black hair stuck out all over. He hadn't even bothered to fix it since the life-and-death chase in our hotel a few hours ago. He was usually so picky about his hair. Mick looked sad too. They both had been good friends with Bruce.

Bruce had been killed hours ago. Shot.

And he'd been trying to guard me.

My vision blurred. I blinked hard and looked at the floor.

"Come on." Mom nudged my arm. "We're all meeting in my dressing room."

Mick and Wendell flanked her as she walked away.

Usually we don't have to be so careful backstage. It's a heavily guarded area anyway. But tonight nothing was the same.

Kim and I followed Mom down a long hall to her dressing room. Morrey, Kim's boyfriend and Rayne's drummer, caught up with us. He put a tattoo-covered arm around Kim, her head only reaching his shoulders. Morrey looked at me and winked, but I saw no happiness in it.

Ross Blanke, the band's tour production manager, hustled up to us, along with Stan, lead guitarist, and Rich, Rayne's bass player.

"Hey." Ross put a pudgy hand on Mom's shoulder. "You're doing great." He waved an arm. "All of you, you're doing just great."

"You do what you have to," Stan said grimly. His black face shone with sweat.

We all trudged into the dressing room. Mick and Wendell took up places on each side of the door.

Marshall, the makeup and hair stylist, started handing out water bottles. In his thirties, Marshall has buggy eyes and curly dark hair. His fingers are long and narrow, and he's great with his makeup tools. But until two days ago, he'd been second to Mom's main stylist, Tom.

"Thanks." I took a bottle from Marshall and tried to smile. Didn't work. Just looking at him made me sad, because his presence reminded me of Tom's absence.

Tom, my closest friend on tour, had been murdered two days ago.

Mom, Ross, Rich, and I sank down on the blue couch — one of the furniture pieces Mom requested in every dressing room. This one was extra large, with a high back and thick arms. To our left stood a table with lots of catered food, but no one was hungry. I'd hardly eaten in the last day and a half and knew I should have something. But no way, not now.

Stan, Morrey, and Kim drew up chairs to form a circle.

"All right." Ross sat with his short, fat legs apart, hands on his thighs. The huge diamond ring on his right hand was turned to one side. He straightened it with his pinky finger. "I've checked outside past the guarded area. The zoo's double what it usually is. The news has already hit, and every reporter and his brother is waiting for us. Some paparazzi are already there, and others have probably hopped planes and will show up by the time we leave."

Is Cat here? I shuddered. The slinky-looking photographer had pulled a fire alarm in our San Jose hotel the night before just to force us out of our rooms. The police told him not to get within five hundred feet of us. Like he'd care.

My eyes burned, and I was so tired. I slumped down in the couch and laid my head back.

Ross ran a hand through his scraggly brown hair. "Fans out there are gonna be talking about what they heard on the news before the concert. Rayne, you should say something about it."

"Yeah." Mom sighed.

Rich frowned. He was moving his shaved head side to side, stretching his neck. His piercing gray eyes looked my way, and his face softened. I looked away.

Everyone was being so nice. Still, it was hard to know three people had died because of me.

Ross scratched his chin. "We got extra coverage from Denver police at the hotel tonight. Tomorrow we head for Albuquerque. It's close enough for Vance to drive the main bus without a switch-off driver, and the next two venues are close too. But we've all been through a lot. Can you guys keep performing?" He looked around, eyebrows raised.

"Man." Morrey raked back his shoulder-length black hair. "If three deaths in two days isn't enough to make us quit ..." His full lips pressed together.

I glanced hopefully at Mom. *Yeah, let's go home!* I could sleep in my own bed, hide from the paparazzi and reporters, hang out with my best friend, Brittany

But canceling concerts would mean losing *a lot* of money. The Rayne tour was supposed to continue another four weeks.

Mom leaned forward, elbows on her knees and one hand to her cheek. Her long red fingernails matched the color of her lips. "I almost lost my daughter tonight." Her voice was tight. "I don't care if I *never* tour again — Shaley's got to be protected. That's the number one thing."

I want you protected too, Mom.

"Absolutely," Morrey said, "but at least the threat to Shaley is gone now that Jerry's dead."

Kim spread her hands. "I don't know what to say. I'm still reeling. We barely had time to talk about any of this tonight before getting onstage. I feel like my mind's gonna explode. And Tom ..."

She teared up, and that made me cry. Kim had been like a mother to Tom. Crazy, funny Tom. It was just so hard to believe he was gone.

I wiped my eyes and looked at my lap.

"Anyway." Kim steadied her voice. "It's so much to deal with. I don't know how we're going to keep up this pace for another month."

Mom looked at Ross. "We can't keep going very long with only Vance to drive the main bus."

Ross nodded. "Until Thursday. I'd have to replace him by then."

"With who?" Mom's voice edged.

"I don't know. I'll have to jump on it."

"You can't just 'jump on it.' We need time to thoroughly check the new driver out."

"Rayne." Ross threw her a look. "I *did* check Jerry out. Completely. He had a false ID, remember? That's what the police said. I couldn't have known that."

"You might have known if you'd checked harder."

Ross's face flushed. "I *did* — "

"No you didn't! Or if you did it wasn't good enough!" Mom pushed to her feet and paced a few steps. "Something's mighty wrong if we can't even find out a guy's a convicted felon!"

What? I stiffened. "How do you know that?"

Mom waved a hand in the air. "The police told me just before we left the hotel."

I stared at Mom. "When was he in prison?"

Mom threw a hard look at Ross. "He'd barely gotten out when we hired him."

Heat flushed through my veins. I snapped my gaze toward the floor. Jerry's last words rang in my head. *Your father sent me.*

My father had purposely sent someone who'd been in prison?

Carter House Girls Series from Melody Carlson

Mix six teenage girls and one '60s fashion icon (retired, of course) in an old Victorian-era boarding home. Add boys and dating, a little high school angst, and throw in a Kate Spade bag or two ... and you've got the Carter House Girls, Melody Carlson's new chick lit series for young adults!

Mixed Bags

Book One

Stealing Bradford

Book Two

Homecoming Queen

Book Three

Viva Vermont!

Book Four

Lost in Las Vegas

Book Five

New York Debut

Book Six

Spring Breakdown

Book Seven

Last Dance

Book Eight

Available in stores and online!